Seriously
Wicked

Tor Books by Tina Connolly

Ironskin
Copperhead
Silverblind
Seriously Wicked

Seriously Wicked

—☾—

TINA CONNOLLY

TOR
TEEN

A TOM DOHERTY ASSOCIATES BOOK
NEW YORK

SERIOUSLY WICKED

A Tor Teen Book
Published by Tom Doherty Associates, LLC
175 Fifth Avenue
New York, NY 10010

www.tor-forge.com

Tor® is a registered trademark of Tom Doherty Associates, LLC.

The Library of Congress Cataloging-in-Publication Data is available upon request.

ISBN 978-0-7653-7516-2 (hardcover)
ISBN 978-1-4668-8074-0 (e-book)

Tor Teen books may be purchased for educational, business, or promotional use. For information on bulk purchases, please contact the Macmillan Corporate and Premium Sales Department at 1-800-221-7945, extension 5442, or write to specialmarkets@macmillan.com.

First Edition: May 2015

Printed in the United States of America

0 9 8 7 6 5 4 3 2 1

For Mom, who is totally not Seriously Wicked

Seriously Wicked

1

True Witchery

I was mucking out the dragon's garage when the witch's text popped up on my phone.

BRING ME A BIRD

"Ugh," I said to Moonfire. "Here we go again." I shoved the phone in my jeans and went back to my broom. The witch's ringtone cackled in my pocket as I swept.

Moonfire looked longingly at the scrub brush as I finished. "Just a few skritches," I told her. "You know what the witch is like." I grabbed the old yellow bristle brush and rubbed her scaly blue back. My phone cackled insistently and I pulled it out again.

HANG SNAKESKINS OUT TO DRY

FEED AND WALK WEREWOLF PUP

MUCK OUT DRAGON'S QUARTERS

DEFROST SHEEP

Done all those, I texted back. *Been up since 5 AM.* Out loud I added, "Get with the program," but I did not text that.

The phone cackled back immediately.

DONT BE SNARKY

THESE ARE CHORES BY WHICH ONE MUST

    UNDERSTAND TRUE WITCHERY

NOW BRING ME A BIRD

"Sorry, Moonfire," I said. "The witch is in a mood." At least she hadn't asked me about the spell I was supposed to be learning. I stowed the brush on a shelf and hurried out the detached RV garage and back into the house. Thirteen minutes to get to the bus stop, to get to school on time. I threw my backpack on as I crossed to the witch's old wire birdcage sitting in the living room window. Our newly acquired goldfinch was hopping around inside. The witch had lured him in with thistle seeds. "C'mon, little guy," I said, and carried the cage up the steps of the split-level to the witch's bedroom.

The witch was sitting up in bed as I knocked and entered. Sarmine Scarabouche is sour and pointed and old. Nothing ever lives up to her expectations. She is always immaculate, with a perfect silver bob that doesn't dare get out of place. Her nightgown is white, the bed is white, the sheets, the walls—everything. She spritzes her whole room with unicorn hair sanitizer every morning so it stays spotless. It's deranged.

"Put the bird on the table, Camellia," she said. "Did you finish this morning's work sheet?"

I plopped down on a white wicker stool, fished out three sheets of folded paper from my back pocket, and passed the top one to her. "The Dietary Habits of Baby Rocs—regurgitation, mostly."

Her sharp eyes scanned the page. "Passable. And the Spell for Self-Defense? Have you made *any* progress?"

The question I had been dreading. I unfolded the second sheet from my pocket while the witch studied me.

Because here's the thing: trying to learn spells is The Worst.

In the first place, spells look like the most insane math problems you've ever seen. Witches are notoriously paranoid, so every spell starts with a list of ingredients (some of which aren't even used) and then has directions like this:

Step 1: Combine the 3rd and 4th ingredients at a 2:3 ratio so the amount is double the size of the ingredient that contains a human sensory organ.

In this case, the ingredient that contained a human sensory organ was pear. P-*ear*.

Har de har har.

That's the only part I've managed to figure out, and I've been carrying around this study sheet for four months now.

The witch looks at these horrible things and just understands them, but then again, she's a witch. Which brings me to reason two why I hate this.

I'm *not* a witch.

Maybe I have to live with her, but I'm never going to be like her. There was no way I could actually work this spell, so Sarmine's trying to make me solve it was basically a new way to drive me nuts.

"Well, it's progressing," I said finally. "Say, what are you going to do with that bird? You aren't going to hurt him, are you?"

The witch looked contemptuously down her sharp nose at me. "Of course not. This is merely another anti-arthritis spell, which will probably work just as well as the last forty-seven I've tried." She drew out a tiny down feather from the white leather fanny pack she wore even in bed, clipped a paper clip on the end, and held it out to me. "Please place this feather in the cage." She picked up her brushed-aluminum wand from the bedside table.

"Isn't this a phoenix feather?" I asked as I obeyed. "I thought you couldn't work magic on those."

"But I can on a paper clip," she said. She touched her wand to a pinch of cayenne pepper from her fanny pack, flicked it at the cage, and the paper-clipped feather rose in the air. It stayed there, hovering.

I tried to remember what some long-ago study sheet had said about phoenix feathers. Very potent, I thought. Had a habit of doing something unexpected, like—

The feather burst into flame.

The goldfinch shot to the ceiling of the cage, startled.

"Watch out!" I said.

The paper-clipped feather levitated and began chasing the finch. The finch cheeped and darted. The flaming feather maneuvered until it was chasing the bird in tight clockwise circles.

"You said you weren't going to hurt it," I shouted, moving toward the cage.

"Back away," said the witch, leveling her wand at me. "I need sixty-three rotations of finch flight to work my spell."

I knew what damage the wand could do. The witch was fond of casting punishments on me whenever I didn't live up to her bizarre standards of True Witchery. Like once I refused to hold the neighbor's cat so she could permanently mute its meow, and she turned me into fifteen hundred worms and made me compost the garden.

But the finch was frightened. A fluff of feather fell and was ashed by the fire. Another step toward the cage . . .

The witch pulled a pinch of something from her pack and dipped her wand in it. "Pins and needles," she said.

"Pardon?"

"If at any time you start to disobey me today, random body parts will fall asleep."

"Oh, really?" I said politely. "How will the spell know?" One foot sneaked closer to the cage, down where the witch couldn't see.

"Trust me, it'll know," Sarmine said, and she flicked the wand at me, just as I took another step.

My foot went completely numb and I stumbled. "Gah!" I said, shaking it to get the blood flowing again. "Why are you so awf—?" I started to say, but then I saw her reach for her pouch and I instead finished, "er, so *awesome* at True Witchery?

It's really amazing. It's taken me all this time to figure out just one ingredient in the self-defense spell."

The wand lowered. Sarmine eyed me. "Which one did you figure out?"

"Pear." I didn't say it very confidently, but I said it.

She considered me. I thought a smile flickered over her angular face. But the next moment it was gone.

Still, she did not raise the wand again.

I breathed and shook my foot some more. I might get to school on time.

"Camellia," she said, considering. Her manicured fingers tapped the white sheets as she studied me. Even in bed her silver chin-length bob was immaculately in place. "I am going to take over the city."

"Really," I said, with maybe too much sarcasm. I was still on edge about the poor finch, who was cheeping like a frightened metronome. But seriously, the witch was always coming up with new plans to take over the city. The last one involved placing a tank of sharks in the courthouse.

Her fingers tapped the wand but it did not lift toward me. She merely said, "Impertinence. Turn off your selective listening and hear me out. It's time we witches reclaimed the world and came out of hiding at last. I have the most magnificent plan yet to control the city. But first, I need a demon."

"A demon?" That was serious. "Don't you think you should go back to sharks?"

"A demon," said the witch firmly. "I shall put his spirit into the plastic mannequin in the basement. The scheme is perfect. I'm summoning him this very afternoon, so I need you to bring me two ounces of goat's blood to lock him into the mannequin."

She eyed me like I was going to complain about where to

find goat's blood, but goat's blood is *sooo* old news. I've got a supplier. I was more concerned about this demon nonsense. "Anything else?" I said. The pins-and-needles feeling was finally wearing off and I could stand on two feet again.

"Three fresh roses, a dried pig's ear, and two spears of rhubarb. Recite for me the properties of rhubarb, please."

Um. That was just on a study sheet a week ago. "Used for stiffening, sharpening, etching. So frequently used in blinding spells that it was once declared contraband by the Geneva Coven. Also good in pies," I said.

A fractional nod that meant approval. "And goat's blood?"

Hells. "Also good in pies?" I said.

An odd line of disappointment crossed her brow. "Camellia, you really have to learn this," she said. "All witches must be able to protect themselves."

I gritted my teeth against this ridiculous statement. No matter how often I reminded her I was never going to be a witch, it didn't make a dent. I was not going to waste another morning arguing. Especially not when the third sheet of paper in my pocket was my study sheet for today's algebra test, and I had had zero time to study it due to snakeskin-hanging and sheep-defrosting and everything else.

The witch took out two crisp twenties from her fanny pack and handed them to me. "Very well, you may go."

I took one step to the door, then turned. "Do you promise you'll release the finch as soon as he's flown far enough?"

A flicker of the eyelid that was the equivalent of a major eye roll. "Yes, Camellia. What use would I have for a goldfinch? It would have to be fed, and it wouldn't provide me with anything useful, like dragon tears or werewolf hairs."

"Or free labor," I muttered under my breath as I left the room.

I hurried out the front door and down the street toward the city bus stop. I'm usually the only one catching this particular bus, but today I noticed a boy in blue jeans standing there, scribbling in a notebook.

I slowed to a walk, trying to remember what I had read about demons. A tank of rabid sharks was one thing, but real demons were a nightmare. I knew that from the WitchNet.

You wouldn't think it, but witches were very early adopters of the Internet. Like I mean by 1990, every single one of them was on, so there's a huge network of information with everyone putting up their How I Made Some Dude Fall in Love with Me spells and so on. It's not the same as the regular Internet, though. Witches are paranoid, and so just like their spellbooks, their sites have warding spells, attack spells, spell programs that change the spell recipe to be wrong if the site decides not to share with you—fun things like that. Digging for information on sensitive topics can be dangerous if you get far off the beaten path.

The witch won't get me a normal-person cell phone—mine only connects to other witches and the WitchNet so I can learn more about True Witchery, blah blah. I would have to spend some time looking up demons today to figure out how to stop the witch this time. It seemed like I'd read something on Witchipedia about demon-stopping once. . . . All I could remember about demons was that, A) they were fire elementals, and B) they didn't like being fire elementals. Their entire goal in life was to take over a human and warp them to their wicked will so they could stay on earth, and yes, I learned all that from the witch's favorite show about demon hunters.

The boy at the bus stop did not look up as I approached. I still didn't recognize him—perhaps he was a junior or senior I'd somehow missed. He had earbuds in and was muttering something, then scribbling furiously. It sounded vaguely like

"cool stick of butter," which seemed unlikely, unless he was trying to remember his grocery list. I got all the way to the stop
before he glanced up—and right through me. He hummed as
he looked back down.

I'm not super-vain, but I have to admit I felt a little miffed
at that. I mean, he was tall and all—probably taller than me,
which was nice, and somewhat rare. And okay, he was cute.
But he wasn't *my* kind of cute. He looked like he belonged in
a boy band, with floppy blond hair and a sweet face. I like them
dark and brooding, like Zolak the demon hunter, who wears
leather pants with zippers all over them.

The bus was coming up the street. If I pulled out my algebra
study sheet, I could get ten minutes of cramming in on the
bus.

And then I saw a small yellow thing zip down the sidewalk
and go right past my head. The finch.

Behind it was the flaming feather.

The witch had let the finch go, as promised. But she hadn't
bothered to catch the feather.

The finch zoomed around us, going right past the boy-band-
boy's face, and the boy even looked up at that. He pulled out his
earbuds, searching for the dive-bombing bird.

I had to catch that feather. The bird streaked past us again,
diving and dodging. I swung and missed.

"Is that your pet bird?" he said. "Can I help you catch it?"

"Not exactly," I said, grabbing at the feather again.

"What—wait, is there something chasing it?"

I lunged again, and this time I caught the feather. Turning
so my back was to the boy, I blew on the feather until the flame
went out. Smother it, I thought, and shoved it into my back
pocket. I whirled around to find the boy looking at me with a
puzzled expression.

"That looked like a flaming feather," he said.

"No, it wasn't," I said. "It was a bumblebee. I didn't want it to sting the bird. I'm against that sort of thing." When you're enslaved to a wicked witch, you end up thinking fast to keep all the weird witchy things a secret. Not always *good* fast, but fast. "Look, isn't that our bus?"

I hurried past the blond boy to where Oliver the bus driver was opening the door for us. Oliver waved at me as I put my foot on the stair. He's a good guy. He waits for me if he sees me running, and I bring him the witch's secret windshield-washing formula when it's sleeting. (Vinegar with three drops of dragon milk; he always says it's just like magic, but he doesn't know the half of it.) I like Oliver, and also I feel you should be extra-pleasant to someone if you plan to bring goat's blood and turtle shells and live roosters onto their nice bus.

"Hi, Oliver," I said, waving back.

"Behind you, Cam," he said. "I think that boy's trying to get your attention."

I turned around to find the boy-band boy making wild fanning gestures at my rear end. "Excuse me?" And then I realized that my butt was really quite warm. A thin trail of smoke was coming from my back pocket.

The feather.

Oh hells. I fanned my rear end desperately, but the smoke only thickened.

"Sorry about this," the boy-band boy muttered. He uncapped his water bottle and doused the rear of my jeans. Water soaked me down to my ankles. I gasped.

He looked both hopeful and apologetic, the same expression Wulfie the werewolf cub gets when he tries to bring in the newspaper and chews it to bits.

It is not often that my wits completely desert me, but they did then. There is no appropriate thing to say to someone who has just emptied his water bottle on your rear end to save you from going up in magical flames. Well, "thank you," I suppose. A very squeaky sort of "thank you" came out as I tottered past the wide-eyed gaze of Oliver and sat down on the next-to-last seat left on the bus. Humiliation and anger at the witch warred inside me. How could I keep people from finding out about my weird home life if the witch insisted on sending flying flaming feathers to my bus stop?

Unfortunately, the very last seat on the bus was right next to me. That's where boy-band boy sat. He looked down at me cautiously, like he wasn't sure if I was pleased or upset with him.

Inanely I said, "Very hot bumblebees they have this time of year. Liable to burst into flame at any moment."

He looked at me, and I honestly could not tell if he was as stumped for words as I was, or if he just thought I was the craziest person he had ever met. I mean, really, what *do* you say to that?

Slowly, he reached up and put his earbuds in.

Embarrassment flooded me and I stared out the window all the way to school. I didn't even remember to look at my soaking-wet study sheet for algebra.

Jenah found me in the girls' locker room, drying my butt under a hand dryer and flipping like crazy through my algebra text-book with the other hand. "Oh, honey," she said, beelining to me. Jenah is my best friend and lockermate, and she would be my confidante if I dared have one of those. She's tiny and trim and Chinese, third generation. Her parents fancy themselves rebellious punk-rocker types, and they encourage her to express herself, whether that means changing the colored streaks she clips into her hair or obsessing about the auras she claims to see around everybody. She says the auras help her tune into the universe—sure, whatever. When you've got a dragon in your garage, you're in no position to judge.

Today Jenah was all in black and pink and bracelets, and her black, asymmetric, partly shaved bob thing had a clipped-in pink streak. She is so chic, so *herself*, it hurts. My hair is kind of nutmeg, my eyes are kind of blue, my nose is kind of shapeless. Whereas Jenah looks like the epitome of Jenah, someone so perfectly who she is that she's untouchable. One of those girls whom everybody already knows, even if we're only in tenth. Jenah would never end up with crispy jeans, witch or no. She commandeered a mini-hairdryer from a freshman on the swim team and turned up the heat on my butt.

"Back to your blush brush," she ordered the Freshman. "I've got news," she said to me, over the dryer.

"Well? Spill."

"Happy to," said Jenah. "Just as soon as you share some information with me." She flicked back her pink lock of hair. "What color is Aunt Sarmine's bedspread?"

Seven years of best friendship and Jenah had never once seen the inside of my house or met the witch. I told everyone I lived with my aunt, because it was easier than explaining the truth about how the witch tricked me out of my loving parents' arms before I was even born. Once when I was eight I looked up all the Hendrixes in the phone book (there were four) and spent the next month of Saturdays taking the bus to each house to ask politely if a witch had stolen a daughter from them—an adorable baby girl with nutmeg hair and a smudge of a nose.

Three of them laughed and one sicced his chihuahua on me.

Anyway, it was one of Jenah's goals in life to see inside my house and meet Aunt Sarmine. I told her she needed better goals, but she went on about keeping our friendship aura tuned by understanding my living space. Or something.

"Her bedspread is white with embroidered golden bumble-bees," I said. That was true. For a megalomaniac witch who made spells with goat's blood, Sarmine could be pretty particular. "Now spill."

Jenah clicked off the hair dryer and tossed it back to the ninth grader. "New boy in our grade," Jenah said to me. "Quiet. Has potential. I think you could nab him if you move fast."

"Not interested," I said. "Too busy. I'm over the whole boy thing. I only date college men. I only date hot-dog vendors. I only date aliens from Neptune."

Jenah laughed appreciatively.

"Do you know if Kelvin's back from his bout with the pig flu?" I said. Kelvin was a total 4-H nerd—and an excellent goat's blood supplier.

"Ew, I do not keep tabs on mustard-aura Kelvin," said Jenah.

"You have him in drama! He gets up and recites monologues about milking cows or whatever. How can you not know?"

"Mustard-aura," repeated Jenah. We left the locker room, and strolled down the hall to First Hour Algebra II. Except we were running late, so it was a fast stroll. School had been back in session long enough for the walls to be well papered—fliers for clubs, posters for some school play, and the ubiquitous school-spirit banners in our stunning colors of orange and forest green. Outside the algebra room, a flyer for Blogging Club was papered over with one for Vlogging Club, and over that, one for the Halloween Dance. "So you'll be okay with going solo to that on Friday?" said Jenah.

"Yuck," I said. "Why do we have a Halloween dance anyway? Who wants to celebrate that?"

"Halloween is super-important," said Jenah. She flicked back her hair as we neared the classroom. "It's a time when you can commune with spirits. Ghosts. Demons."

I shuddered. "You wouldn't be so fond of demons if you

thought they actually existed," I said. "Just like it's real easy to think witches are cool if you haven't actually met them."

"Witches?" she said, with an eyebrow.

"Or whatever. You know."

I pushed open the scarred wooden door and Jenah hissed behind me. "There he is. Go get him, tiger!"

'Course, you all know what happened next.

Sitting in the desk next to mine was a sweet-faced boy-band boy who, at the sight of me and my dry jeans, blushed red-hot pink to the tips of his perfectly shaped ears.

2

In a Pig's Ear

It wasn't the fault of the red-eared boy-band boy sitting next to me during Algebra II. I flunked the algebra test all on my own merits.

Okay, maybe I didn't flunk, but there's no way I did better than a 70, which was practically as bad. As long as I maintained my A's, teachers didn't get too upset when the witch didn't come in for parent conferences. But a C-minus? If I went downhill in algebra, then good old Rourke would be calling Sarmine Scarabouche on the phone, and wouldn't that just go over well. The witch had never come to a single thing at school my entire life and I planned to make sure it stayed that way.

The others streamed out the door as I pushed my way to Rourke's desk in the back corner. "Mr. Rourke?" I said. He wore way-too-thin button-down shirts that'd been washed too many times. Jenah called him Mr. Visible Undershirt, sometimes too loudly.

"What is it, Camellia?"

"Mr. Rourke," I said again. Here's where Jenah would study his aura and see how to butter him up, but for good or bad, I was a straight shooter. "I know I sucked on that test. Can I do some extra credit to make up?"

"I don't give out extra credit willy-nilly," said Rourke, nudging the tests into a perfect stack. His four red pens were horizontal at the top of his laminated desk. A full two-liter of off-brand root beer stood capped on the corner, and an empty one fizzed off a faint sarsaparilla smell from the plastic waste-basket. I thought he must be lonely.

"Okay, what else could I do?" I said. "Could I study more and retake it? I know I'm not hopeless at math. I had A's in Algebra One and Geometry. Algebra Two is just kinda . . . mysterious."

Rourke scratched his whiskery chin. "You could come after school and work with our tutor. If I see improvement, I *might* consider some extra credit."

"Awesome," I said. "I'll be in tomorrow."

"Today," said Rourke. "He only comes on Tuesdays and Thursdays."

"I can't today," I said.

Rourke flipped through the tests till he found mine. Without even needing an answer sheet, he went through, x-ing out my work with a thick red felt tip.

"Er. I thought we got credit for showing our work?"

Rourke drew another set of red *X*'s. "If it's good work," he said. He flipped back to the front, capped his first red pen and chose a different one from the lineup. This one was a lurid red-orange and smelled like rubbing alcohol. In slow motion it wrote a very decisive "61%" next to my name. "You know, I have been looking forward to meeting your aunt," Rourke said. "I hear she is a very striking woman."

Cold dread iced my spine. "I'll see you after school," I said.

With Mr. Visible Undershirt commandeering my after-school hour, I was going to have to sneak out at lunch to get the witch's errands done.

That is, if I should *do* her errands.

I spent all of Second Hour French considering that conundrum. Usually when the witch ordered items, I jumped. For example, once I failed to find elf toenails for her. (I still haven't found anybody who supplies them, for that matter. The witch refuses to admit that certain ingredients might be mythical.) For punishment the witch turned me into a solar panel salesman and made me go around to every house in a half-mile radius and lecture about alternative forms of enérgy.

Now I considered my foot. Losing one foot for a few moments this morning wasn't the end of the world. I had stumbled, but I was still here. But what was going to come after that? Both legs? My body? My heart? I shuddered.

Despite what the witch had said, I didn't *think* her spell could read my thoughts. It definitely knew when I acted against her—the step toward the birdcage had proved that. But thinking?

I clenched my fist and thought hard, *I am not going to help the witch summon a demon.*

Nothing happened. Well, there were some pins and needles in my fist, but only because I was clenching it so hard. Slowly I relaxed.

Okay, then. A plan blossomed. I would gather her ingredients, and then, at the very last possible second, I would destroy them. As long as I didn't chicken out.

My phone vibrated in my backpack and I sneaked it out under cover of my desk.

PLANETS PERFECT @3:45

WILL SUMMON GREAT & NEFARIOUS ESTAHOTH >:-(

DON'T FORGET GOAT'S BLOOD

OR ELSE

Or else. *Or else.* I sighed. Everything falling asleep would still come, but later. The witch would come up with some worse punishment on top of that. Really, all I was doing was delaying my misery from right now until the end of the school day.

"Mademoiselle Hendrix? *Comment dit-on* dilemma *en fran-çais?*"

"*Un dilemme,*" I said. "*Un dilemme.*"

The school gave us an entire eighteen minutes to eat lunch, which was just enough time to get to one location: across the street to the specialty grocery, Celestial Foods. Which meant I couldn't eat lunch with Jenah or track down Kelvin for the goat's blood. I stuck a note on her half of the locker that said, "please please PLEASE find Kelvin during A Lunch and tell him I'll pay double for two ounces of the usual, *today,* I owe you BIG-TIME," grabbed my emergency jar of peanut butter, and dashed down the hall to the side exit.

In theory it's a closed campus, but in practice the security guys are always busy busting up smokers in the parking lot on the other side of the school, so as long as you're subtle, you can sneak out the side door, through the overgrown elms.

I ate my peanut butter lunch while I headed to the store. It was a lovely October day, full of blue skies and red rustling maple leaves. My mind started to clear. I was going to get the witch's ingredients, and then destroy them at the last possible second. Spill her tea on them—whoops! Explode them in the microwave. Something.

But that might not be enough to stop the witch.

Her taking-over-the-world plans tended to be pretty determined. I mean, surely the planets would align again tomorrow or Friday or something, right? She was theoretically capable of purchasing her own ingredients for the spell, even if I'd never seen her set foot in anything so common as a *grocery store*.

I needed to know how to stop the demon in case she got one summoned.

I pulled up Witchipedia on my phone. I had been about to
look up demons this morning when I'd seen that new boy at my
bus stop. My face got warm, thinking about it. I had been rude
and awkward, and I did not like to think of myself as a rude,
awkward person. I would find him and apologize. Maybe, too,
I could ask him what he was listening to, and if the humming
and scribbling meant he truly *was* a boy-band boy, because that
would be kind of cool . . .

Ahem.

Demons. Witchipedia. Right.

I found:

> *Demon* (disambiguation). *Demon* may refer to:
>> **Chad Demon**, an embodied demon and WitchNet
>> personality best known for a series of spoofs of American
>> (nonwitch) TV shows
>>
>> ***Demons! The Musical***, at three years, two months
>> the longest-running witch show without the cast simul-
>> taneously exploding into paranoia and quitting
>>
>> **Elemental** obsessed with finding embodiment (aka a
>> human soul and body to keep). Neutrality of this article
>> is disputed.

It continued on from there, but I clicked on the "Elemental"
article. A summoned demon had to have a living form to inhabit
in order to spend time on earth. Once inside a body, demons
became very tricky. Using a variety of techniques (see *techniques*), they could steal most humans' souls in less than a week.
A demon who obtained a soul could not be sent home, even
when its contract was completed. It would keep the body for the
rest of the body's mortal life span. Witches untrained in demon
summoning were advised to reconsider, as demons on the loose
could cause chaos, plague, destruction, blah blah . . .

I bookmarked that section of the page to read later. Witches predicting terrible results tend to get wordy and melodramatic. The witch had said she was putting this demon in a mannequin, so I didn't need to worry about demons eating souls.

I just needed to know how to stop the demon from fulfilling the witch's latest city-taking-over plan.

The stoplight turned green just as I reached the crossing to the shopping center and I hurried across, skimming for the section on how to stop demons. Ah, here. The best way to stop a demon, it said, is—

And that's when a tall girl burst out of nowhere, jostling my elbow and knocking my peanut butter to the sidewalk. I grabbed for it and my phone went flying. The plastic peanut butter jar cracked as it hit the curb. The phone hit the sidewalk and skittered across the cement.

The screen went blank. "Oh hells!" I growled at it.

The girl whirled, clutching a paper bag. "Watch where you're going."

"Me? It was *you*! Oh. Sparkle."

Sparkle was a junior, the sort that trailed even seniors in her wake. Half Japanese/half white, nearly as tall as me, and pretty even before the nose job. She was in a long shimmery skirt and beaded jersey top; as usual she looked too glamorous for school. It wasn't a look any other girl could've carried off, though a few of her clueless followers tried, with predictably hilarious results.

"Camellia," she said with equal distaste. "Didn't grow into your nose over the summer, I see."

"At least it's my own nose," I said.

Sparkle pounced on that, paranoia sharp in her voice. "I never—What have you heard?" Her fingers felt along her newly straightened nose. "Are people talking about it? It's all lies. It just . . . happened."

"Oh, please," I said. "At least get a better cover story." I picked up my broken peanut butter and cell phone. The display was scratched. I pressed the "power" button, hoping it would turn on without the coaxing of dragon milk.

Sparkle's lips tightened and she clutched the coral cameo she always wore. "Do you still want to be a magic witchy-poo when you grow up?"

For the record, there's nothing worse than having a dead friendship with the top girl in school. A girl who's so top that if she wants to wear sequins and go by the name of Sparkle, girls go cross-eyed with jealousy and think it's cool. We were best friends when I was five and she was six and I didn't know better. I just remember a time when I thought she was the most awesome girl in the world and we spent every single second together.

Told each other all our secrets.

Sneaked down to the basement to watch the witch work a secret, *nasty* spell . . .

I shuddered at the memory. My stupid innocence back then meant this skinny, black-haired, *glittery* girl knew way too much.

Sparkle watched me cringe at her words. Her mouth softened, opened to say something.

"I think there's an ant in my peanut butter," I said.

Sparkle stopped whatever she'd been going to say. She looked down her straightened nose at me and the sneer returned. "Don't let me keep you from your shopping, *Cash*." My old nickname on her lips cut me to the quick.

"I won't, Miss Smells-to-the-Left." The childish insult rolled delightfully off my tongue.

As she stalked off I wondered exactly what she was doing over here. Her paper bag looked like it had Celestial Foods' logo. I leaped to a range of improbable ideas, but then I shook my head. The only reason I was suspicious about other people's doings was because I was always hiding things.

Normal people didn't have to learn about the properties of rhubarb and where to source juniper berries and grapeseed oil.

Normal people got normal food at the grocery store.

I hurried into Celestial Foods, snagging three pinky-white roses from a galvanized watering can by the front door. They dripped on my shoe as I wound brown paper around their bottoms. First ingredient—check.

Next, the fresh produce section, where Alphonse, the son of the owner, was stacking pyramids of squash. Alphonse was a college boy, but not the kind of college boy that makes you wonder if you should pretend to know how to do a keg stand if suddenly called upon to demonstrate. (I mean, he's cute and all, but he doesn't leer, and I've never once heard him say "woooooooo.") He had black dreads to his butt and vegan sandals and he was majoring in environmental engineering because Celeste thought that was a positive career path, but really he just wanted to be one of those people who sneaks into labs and sets all the rabbits and monkeys free.

"Heya, Cam," he said. "What are you trying to track down this time?"

"A weird one today," I said. "One pig's ear." The moment it came out of my mouth I remembered to whom I was talking and my stomach fell. A pig's ear! Alphonse would never forgive me.

Except he nodded and said, "Good timing. We just got a batch in." He hollered over his shoulder to the back of the store, "Hey, Mom, can you bring Cam a pig's ear?" He turned back to me and my open mouth and said, "Right time of year for them. Anything else?"

"Well, um. Rhubarb?" I said. I wondered how you could have a wrong time of year for pig's ears. I turned around, looking for where the rhubarb had been before. Except . . . it wasn't. "Oh, man. Is rhubarb out of season now?"

"Trying to stick to locally grown, when we can," said Alphonse. "Flying out-of-season veg around the world is just not good for—"

"I know, I know," I said. Alphonse took everything so personally. "I'm not criticizing. My aunt needs some."

He dragged me down the crammed produce aisle, and I nearly took out a pyramid of spotted apples with my hip. "We have some really nice local pears in. If she's making a pie—"

"Not a pie. She really just wants some rhubarb. Sorry."

"She should've come in September. That was the last of it," he said.

"I got some in September," I said. I tapped an acorn squash thoughtfully. "Does it come any other way?"

"Frozen," he said.

"Yes?"

"But we don't carry that anymore. Our last supplier was caught doing business with people who do business with people who don't compost."

"Did you say your mom was here?" I said.

"Oh, I just remembered we have it canned."

"Thank you." I took the can from Alphonse and trailed him up to the register. I had seven minutes left and it only took six to walk back to school. "How's the eco-work?" I whispered. "Eco-work" for Alphonse covered everything from protesting fracking to sneaking into people's homes to turn off their lights. As long as there was a potentially dangerous situation involved, he was in.

"Not good," he whispered back. "We're trying to liberate some lab animals at the campus, but we can't get an inside man or woman on the job." He considered. "Or a gender-neutral person. Or multiple gendered. I wouldn't want you to think I was being exclusionary."

"I didn't think that," I assured him. "I'm in complete agreement with liberating testing animals. Um, speaking of, do you think your mom was able to find the pig's ear?"

Alphonse moved spaghettied piles of register tape and recycled paper bags as he squeezed behind the register. "Hey, Mom!" he shouted.

Celeste hurried down the cereal aisle, wooden necklaces clacking. Celeste is black and somewhat rounded, and unlike her son, has just a hint of some sort of British in her voice, even though she's lived here since she was like twelve. I'd come to associate Brits with extreme helpfulness and a listening ear over the years, which will probably not be useful if I ever go to England. Celeste pushed her plastic glasses up her nose. "Alphonse, love, we have an intercom."

"Uses electricity," said Alphonse.

"Camellia, darling, it's lovely to see you." Celeste enveloped me in a warm, wool-cardigan hug. Then produced something from her apron pocket. "Here's your pig's ear."

The "pig's ear" was pinky-brown. It had a ruffled, twisty cap and a spongy stem with a bit of dirt on the bottom.

Oh. "Is that a mushroom?"

"Pig's ear mushrooms," she said. "Autumn only, get them while you can. Such a sweet name. I assure you, I'd rather sell mushrooms than real pig's ears." She set the mushroom on my rhubarb can.

"We wouldn't sell real pig's ears," growled Alphonse as he rang me up. "Barbaric, mutilating . . ."

The worst part of that was, I realized then that I didn't like the idea of a real pig's ear either. I'd just been thinking of it as an item to keep the witch off my back and not something that once belonged to a real live animal.

You know how you grow up with something day after day and you're so used to it that you don't realize you don't agree with it till all of a sudden?

Yeah.

I didn't have the nerve to say I was supposed to find a real one, so I paid for the mushroom along with everything else.

"What is your aunt going to do with just one mushroom?" Celeste said.

"Um. Make One-Mushroom Soup?"

Celeste patted my shoulder. "Always good to see you, love. Bring your aunt in here sometime, will you? From the sound of her recipes over the years, I've always thought we must have a lot in common."

"Right. Definitely. Any day now. Just as soon as she gets back from her trip to Nepal. And gets over the chicken pox. And her fear of grocery stores. And learns how to speak English. Very soon now," I said, and flat-out ran back to Fourth Hour American History.

3

Goat's Blood

American History I is the worst class to have after lunch, because if there's anything I'm going to fall asleep over, it's Mrs. Taylor's teaching method of playing ancient VHS tapes where actors explain the Bill of Rights using hip slang. Not that I was going to fall asleep today. I drummed my fingers and worried over whether Kelvin would be able to bike all the way home to his farm and back with the goat's blood in time for the great planetary alignment. Usually the witch gave me a couple days' notice for the weirder stuff, and Kelvin and I did a cooler hand-off. I drummed harder.

My worries were interrupted by the appearance of two notes. First was the best message. A knock on the door and a student brought me a terse printout from Rourke that said: *Tutor sick. Come tomorrow.*

I breathed a sigh of relief and immediately received a second note. This one was on purple paper and was passed across the aisle to me while a tall permed actor said, "Yo, you mean I don't have to give these grody Redcoat soldiers room and board?" The note had been sent by Jenah to Dean to Kyndra (who hissed, "Get a phone!"), and it said: *K says too weak from pig flu to bike. Ugh! Will phone his Mom to bring yr request at 3 PM. Meet under T-Bird. 2bl UGH.*

The T-Bird was the gigantic metal Thunderbird statue, our mascot, perched at the old front entrance to the school. It was up on a big cement block, and its claws extended to grasp a tiny mouse sculpture hidden in the grass. Since the new addition a decade ago, the old statue had gotten overgrown with ivy and shrouded in elms, so the "double-ugh" was in reference to the Thunderbird's reputation as a place for hookups. But I doubted Kelvin paid any attention to things like that, so the super-sexy implications of the T-Bird were not the thing that made my blood run cold.

It was the phoning of the mom.

And the asking her to bring goat's blood.

Now, I didn't know Kelvin's mom up close and personal. But even though she lived on a farm, she was still a mom. What mom wouldn't be weirded out by knowing that her son was marketing goat's blood to some girl at school? Come to that, how did Kelvin have goat's blood around, anyway? I'd never really wanted to know—and now, the more I thought about it, the more it bothered me, like the pig's ear.

At three, I grabbed my stuff from my locker and headed for the Thunderbird statue. The shaded area around the T-Bird was full of boys macking on girls and vice versa. (Boys macking on boys hung out in the theater, and girls macking on girls met in the park.)

Kelvin is tall, white, and wide, and he stands all stifflike. Like a bowling pin. He was shifting from one foot to the other, carefully not looking at a couple sucking face in the ivy near his knees. His deadpan face was moon-pale in the green shadow of the elms. He held a red-and-white mini-cooler.

Behind him, Kelvin's mom waved from the car. She was wide like Kelvin, sporting a baggy red T-shirt, frizzy blond-gray ringlets, and a smear of sunblock down her nose.

She did not look suspicious.

I relaxed and waved back. "Thanks, Kelvin. I owe you big-time." I parked my butt on the concrete base of the T-Bird and pulled out the last of my cash. "I don't have all I promised you but I'll bring the rest tomorrow. You know I'm good for it."

Kelvin took the folded bills and nodded. "Kel-vin is a-ware," he said in the robot voice he used sometimes. He did a lot of things that clearly he found funny, even if nobody else thought so. I was used to it. He set the cooler down on the concrete with a *skritch*.

"Did your mom wonder what was up?" I said.

"I told her you needed it for important witch rituals," said Kelvin, his wide face dead serious.

I nearly fell off the statue base. Then I reminded myself that was Kelvin's sense of humor acting up again. Deadpan didn't even begin to describe it.

"Ha ha," I said. "What did you really say?"

"I told her you needed it for a science project," he said. "Testing it to see what hormones showed up." Robot voice. "Now she thinks you're sma-art."

Another joke, but this one I could handle. "Excellent news. I aim to fool everybody," I joked back. Then I steeled my nerve and asked, "By the way . . . How do you, um, get the goat's blood?"

"Fangs," he said.

I raised eyebrows.

"A syringe, of course. Don't worry, I told Mom your witch rituals needed it to be fresh."

"You're such a kidder," I said weakly.

"Good trade. Robot Kelvin bring you blood, you go to Halloween Dance with him. Together, dance like robots." He improvised a few steps.

Which kind of looked like fun, but my thoughts were elsewhere, jumping ahead to catching the bus with my treasure trove of ingredients. "Smart *and* easily bought by goat's blood,"

I said. "My reputation is improving every second I stand here."
I jumped to the ground, narrowly missing some dude's hand.
"Look, I gotta run or I'll miss my bus. But thanks again." I
punched his shoulder in a friendly fashion and hurried through
clinging couples.

The bus was already loading, so I ran the last twenty feet,
cooler banging. The door stayed open and I swung aboard just
as it pulled off.

Despite the sweaty-boys-on-bus stink, I breathed a little easier. I had everything but the pig's ear, and my only homework
I hadn't finished in class was reading the first two acts of something called *The Crucible*. I could get that done after my evening chores. Maybe I'd read it to Moonfire during her dinner.
She liked being read to, even though I was never sure how much
was lost in translation.

The bus was packed, as usual, but there was one seat left.

A seat saved by a backpack belonging to a tall boy with floppy
blond hair.

"I saw you running, and I thought I owed you one for soaking you this morning." He grinned and a teasing expression
crossed his kind face. "I almost had to fight that football player
for you, so say you forgive me."

"Of course I do," I said, and wondered if it was my turn to
have pink ears. After all, it's not every day a boy says he's willing
to fight a football player to secure you a bus seat, even if it's just
a joke. "And—forgive me, too. I was rude, and I'm sorry." I started
to sit down in the space he made, then stopped. "I'm not on fire
again, am I?"

His eyes flickered down to my jeans and back up. "All clear."

I plopped my backpack and rose bouquet on my lap and set
the mini-cooler between my feet, where I could keep track of
its whereabouts. The orange and yellow trees whisked by outside as the bus lurched toward home. I was going to make it.

Except . . . the pig's ear.

The pig's ear that I didn't want. The pig's ear that I had to get . . . or else.

I sighed.

"What's up?"

"I had a shopping list of stuff my aunt needed today . . . never mind." I drummed my fingers on my jeans, thoughts churning over what to do. If I didn't bring the witch all the ingredients, there would be punishments . . . but I couldn't let her summon the demon . . . "Gah, I give up," I said. "I'm just not going to get the last thing. I'm not."

My earlobe fell asleep. Then a whole patch of my head. I shook my head, trying to get feeling to return.

One thigh went out. A shin down to the ankle. Then all my toes snuffed out, *pop pop pop*—

"Gah, I mean I *am* going to get the stuff, I am," I said, desperately drumming my feet on the bus floor until sensation returned. I snuck a glance at boy-band boy, who seemed tempted to put his earbuds in again. "Sorry. My aunt . . . is kind of demanding. She needs a lot of specific things for her . . . job."

Boy-band boy lowered his earbuds and looked thoughtful. "Does she work for herself?"

"In a manner of speaking. Yeah." I massaged my ear as the pins and needles died away.

He nodded. "My parents ran a no-kill animal shelter in my old town," he said. "My dad ran the place and my mom donated time as a vet. I had to pitch in. You can't blow things off like everyone else can, you know? Not if your parents have a family business. There are dogs to walk. Cats to rub with disgusting flea medicine. Cages to scrub after the cats have scraped all the flea medicine off."

"Up at five every day?" I said.

"Rain or shine."

"Study with one hand, muck out kennels with the other?"

"Sounds like you know the drill."

"Why did you move here?"

He shrugged. "Couldn't ever get enough donations. We finally had to transfer all the animals to the local county shelter and shut down. That was rough . . . well. Mom and Dad wanted a change, and Mom found a new clinic up here." He wound down, looking a little embarrassed about having shared so much. But he had done it out of kindness, trying to empathize with his animal shelter story. It made me warm to him.

Maybe giving him one piece of information was worth the risk. "Do you know where I could get a pig's ear?"

"Like for a dog?"

"Oh!" Why hadn't I thought of that? "Yes," I said.

"There's a pet store in biking distance from our bus stop," he said.

"Right!" I had gotten emergency dog food there once for Wulfie when the witch was in D.C. trying to transform the vice president into a grain elevator.

"But don't bother. I got a whole bag for Bingo the other day after he ate my sneakers. I'll give you one." He cocked his head, the boy-band-boy hair flopping, and it suddenly made him look devilish instead of sweet. "It's the least I can do for soaking you."

Another nice gesture. I could get used to this. "I don't even know you and already I dub you 'The Best,'" I said. "My name's Camellia, but my friends call me Cam."

"Devon."

"So, Devon. Are you in a band?"

He looked startled. "How did you know?"

"You were humming and writing in a notebook this morning," I said. I didn't mention the part about him looking like a boy-band boy. "Songs?"

His eyes lit up. "They just grab you when you're walking

along. Bits of melody, lyrics." He ran his fingers through his hair. "I mean, they're not all equally good . . ."

"Sing one?"

"On the bus?"

"Sure," I said. "Don't musicians like to show off?"

His ears went a little pink, but he closed his eyes and sang in a velvety sort of voice, "She's a cool stick of butter with a warm warm heart . . ."

"So there *was* a stick of butter in it," I said when he stopped.

"What?"

"Is that all there is to the song?"

"So far," he said. "Dad always says the first phrase comes free, but then you have to work on the rest. I used to take my guitar to my old school and sit outside during lunch and work out chording."

"I like it," I said. "So what do you play in your boy band?"

"*Regular* band," he said.

"Regular band. Backup vocals, some guitar?"

"They want me to sing lead but . . . er . . ." He trailed off. "Stage fright."

"Ooh," I said sympathetically. The bus stopped on my street and we got off, heading down the sidewalk toward the witch's house. "Have you tried imagining the audience in their underwear?"

"Oddly enough, that doesn't help." He fiddled with his backpack. "During practice it's great. I mean, we're singing the stuff I wrote, right? It's awesome. It's a rush. And then we get to a concert . . . My voice shakes when I solo and that's all you can hear on the mic. Embarrassing. We're not even famous, you know? Have you heard of Blue Crush?"

I shook my head.

"See? I'm talking backyards, church concerts, talent shows. That's what we've played. Maybe now that I'm an hour away

I should let them find someone new, so they're not stuck with me . . ." He tugged a lock of his floppy blond hair and trailed off. "Well, look. I'll run home and get you that pig's ear, okay? I'm just a block over."

"You're awesome," I said. We stopped in front of my driveway. It's surprising how normal the witch's house looks from the outside: an ugly old split-level in browns and tans, landscaped with thorny bushes that she prunes with a ruler. I didn't know what to say about the stage fright, so I just slugged his shoulder sympathetically. "Oh hey, I know this sounds weird, but don't ring the doorbell, okay?" I made the crazy sign around my temple. "My aunt hates being interrupted. I'll meet you in the driveway in, what, ten minutes?"

Devon nodded. "All right. See you soon, Camellia . . . Cam."

I hummed to myself as I set the roses and cooler on the front porch and dug around for my keys. There was something pretty awesome about a boy singing a song to you, even just one line of a song. I had never particularly thought about boy-band boys before, but perhaps they were beginning to grow on me.

I unlocked the door and Wulfie came tearing out of the house, jumping on me and licking my face. "Down, boy," I said, laughing. He tore off around the yard in joyful circles, going, "arf arf arf," while I hummed. It really was a spectacular fall day. Had the sky ever been this blue? Surely it wasn't just the chat with the boy-band boy making those fall leaves so glorious? I pulled out my phone to take a picture of happy Wulfie plowing through piles of red leaves, and the sight of the scratches all over the phone's surface brought everything flooding right back. Sparkle. Witchipedia.

Demons.

I just needed to know the end of that sentence The best way to stop a demon is . . .

I hit the "power" button a whole bunch, but all that happened was the screen blinked greenly at me through its sidewalk scratches.

Stupid Sparkle.

Luckily, like I said, witches were big on the Internet. We had a kitchen laptop that Sarmine used for recipes, since she cooked dinner. I looked down at the werewolf pup, who was busy looking for a spot to do his business. "Don't go anywhere," I told him sternly, and ran inside. I thunked the laptop down on the yellow laminate counter and flipped it open. Pulled up Witchipedia. Demons, demons . . .

The witch swept into the kitchen, a wave of lavender and lemon cleaner billowing behind her. Hard to tell if that was cleaning or spells. "The planets are aligning gracefully," Sarmine said. "Soon it will be time to summon Estahoth. Are you baking something?"

"Er," I said. I scrolled down the page, scanning.

"Cooking is a waste of your precious time," Sarmine said. "If you have extra time in the afternoons you should apply yourself to learning the spells I set you. A good self-defense spell is every witch's best friend."

This is the point where usually I say, "not a witch," but I didn't want to get sidetracked down that conversation. "Just curious about demons," I said. "You never had me learn about them."

"Camellia," said the witch in her most aggrieved tone, "there are so many things that you have not learned about that we cannot possibly encompass them all in the short time I get with you each day. Now, if you would just apply yourself, or give up going to that useless human school—" She brushed a bit of lint off my shoulder, and I tweaked the laptop so she wouldn't see what I was looking for.

"I love that school; you can't stop me," I said automatically. This was familiar territory and I'd just reached "The best way to stop a demon is . . .

". . . not to summon it."

Hells.

"Of course, today you will watch a most ingenious exhibition of demon-summoning," said the witch, sailing past me to close the open front door. "Perhaps that will finally be the magic to inspire you. This will be an excellent lesson for you to view. I expect this is the goat's blood?"

The ingredients. *I had to destroy the ingredients.*

I lunged for the front door. We reached the cooler at the same time and she scooped it up.

"Repeat after me," said the witch, cradling the cooler and rose bouquet as she returned to the kitchen. "Goat's blood is used for binding, winding, and minding, in processes with tin, and as a substitute for Irish whiskey."

"Um, what about the weather? Have you checked the forecast?"

"The forecast?" Sarmine peered out the kitchen window at the bright blue sky.

I lunged for the cooler, trying to tug it from her arms. "Giant thunderstorms predicted," I panted, even as my ribs fell asleep and then my nose. "Electric interference. Everyone knows . . . don't summon demons . . . in storms . . ."

She was strong, but I was younger and stronger. Her feet skidded, she staggered, her hands slipped off. I stumbled backward on the linoleum, clutching the cooler.

The witch's silver eyebrows drew to a point.

She took a pinch of red powder and a spoonful of bread crumbs from one of the pockets of her fanny pack, spat on her hand, and touched her palm with her wand.

My mind raced, but this time there was no escape. My eyes were frozen, and clever words and maneuvers deserted me. I clutched that cooler tighter.

She flicked the wand at me and my hands turned into cooked noodles.

Seriously. Cooked noodles. Limp and soggy and rippled around the edges, like lasagna. Wobbly orange-painted finger-nails marked their edges. My noodle hands slid right off the cooler handle and the cooler crashed to the linoleum floor.

I squeaked.

"A good self-defense spell would have been your best friend just now," lectured the witch, picking up the cooler. Her heels clicked on the linoleum as she retrieved the fallen rose bouquet and set the roses carefully in a crystal vase full of water. "Why, I remember when I was eight, and a rogue wizard loosed the last orc on earth into our basement . . ." She patted her fanny pack. "But I had my ingredients and my wand! Oh, I was in top form."

I lunged for the roses to destroy that possible ingredient in-stead, but my wobbly noodle hands missed the roses and smacked the crystal vase. The vase toppled over, rolling toward the floor. Self-preservation surged again. What would the witch do to me if I broke her crystal vase? Instinct made me launch my whole body underneath the vase as it fell.

Water soaked me for the second time that day. Rose thorns smacked my face.

But my body broke the vase's fall. I lay on the cool linoleum floor, shaky, my limp noodle hands flopping back and forth.

"Impressive," said the witch, as she grabbed the three roses between thumb and forefinger. Her skin was so dry and dessi-cated that the thorns didn't even draw blood. "Did you remember the rhubarb?"

"Yes," I said from the floor. It smelled like lemon cleaner.

"Very well." Wand flick. "You may have your hands back." The witch turned to the basement steps. "Oh, and Camellia?

Bring the pig's ear down with you. Nasty thing. I don't want to touch it."

Pig's ear. *Pig's ear!* Stupid witch and her stupid, stupid, *evil* things. I was so mad that I forgot all about the werewolf pup in the front yard, and my appointment to meet Devon in the driveway. I ran soaking wet after her and down the cement steps to the basement. "You can't treat me like that!" I shouted. "I'm a person, too, you know!"

Sarmine raised a silver eyebrow.

"And pigs! You can't treat pigs as things to just chop up for your stupid summoning. Pigs are living beings! They have rights, too!"

"Don't drip on my pentagram."

Angry as I was, I did step back at that. If the witch *was* going to summon a demon, I sure didn't want him to escape his pentagram prison. I shoved my wet hair back and glared at the witch, who ignored me. Prickles went up and down my ribs as feeling returned.

The pentagram was a blue chalk outline on the cement floor. It was big enough for several people to stand inside. It had one of our banged-up card table chairs in it, and on the chair was the old mannequin on which the witch usually kept a pointy hat. The mannequin was wearing a faded red T-shirt that said, VOTE HEXAR/SCARABOUCHE 1982. It stared blankly at the wall, its body tilting to the left.

I felt a kinship with the mannequin. It didn't have any idea what was about to be done to it. "I'm a person, too," I muttered again as I scratched my shins.

The witch knelt on the stone floor in her skirt and support hose and ruffled salmon blouse. "Isn't my pentagram lovely?" she said reverently. "I haven't drawn one in ages. Since before you were born." She tapped it with her wand and blew on it gently, but the chalk dust did not budge.

"Why break a winning streak?" I said.

"Last time I summoned a very minor demon. Nikorzeth. He barely had enough power to heal the dragon's broken wing."

No wonder Moonfire kept one wing shuttered closed when the weather turned chill. Maybe if the witch would heat that damn garage for her . . . "Broken wing?"

"That's when I found her," the witch said absently. "She was at the end of a long flight and a storm moved in. She got tangled in a power line. And only another elemental can use magic on a dragon." Sarmine's eyes gleamed as she warmed to her lecture. Gods, that woman loves to lecture. "You know how powerful Moonfire's milk is, and that's just her milk. Why, the list of elementals is one of the first things I taught you. 'Dragon, phoenix, and demon fell; these three a witch cannot bespell.'"

It was cool in the basement, in my damp shirt. I wrapped my arms around my waist. "Why do we call it milk?" I said. "She's a reptile, not a mammal."

"To be precise, she's neither. Elementals are not part of the animal kingdom, as none of the three are mortals which feed on organic matter, as humans and elephants and werewolves do. Moonfire is of the class *Draconis,* which is another thing entirely," said the witch. "But to answer your question more fully, I suppose we call her tear secretions milk because we always have." Sarmine rocked back on her heels and studied her gold bracelet watch. "Three forty-one. We'd better get a move on."

The witch crushed the petals from the three roses with a mini–food processor. She scraped the mixture into a porous stone bowl that usually holds bus tickets. Then she added one drop of dragon milk. The sweet scent of roses mingled with a fiery, coppery, *dragony* smell.

The witch walked around the pentagram three times widdershins and added a chiffonade of basil. Three times back and a pinch of dried salamander from her fanny pack. The salamander dissolved in a gunshot bang and shot up a purple cloud of smoke. My stomach was cold and knotted, and my wet hair hung in chill coils against my neck.

Watching the witch work a spell this dark and complex made me feel sick inside, and a long-ago memory of sneaking downstairs with Sparkle beat against my brain. I swallowed the memory, closed my mind against its darkness. Put my shirtsleeve up to my mouth, trying to clear my breath of the taste of salamander smoke.

"I love the purple smoke part!" shouted the witch. "I hope you're watching, Camellia. Someday I'll teach you all this."

"Not a chance," I said, thinking of all the animals that had to snuff it to make this spell of Sarmine's. "I wouldn't summon a demon for anything. You can't make me into a witch. You can't make me be like you."

The witch's exaltation dissipated and her spine stiffened. "Recipe done," she said shortly, not looking at me. "Now the words."

"Except for the pig's ear, right?" I said. My voice hardly wobbled.

"The what?"

"Except for the pig's ear. I didn't get you the pig's ear. So you can't summon the demon, because you're missing an ingredient."

The witch laughed from deep in her gut, her salmon ruffles shaking. With effort she composed herself. "I shouldn't laugh—it's too ignorant to be funny," she said. She wiped her eyes with a bit of lace and explained, "The pig's ear is for Wulfie to chew on. So he'll stop chewing my good shoes."

A dog toy. A stinking dog toy. "And the rhubarb?"

She shook her head. "'Stiffening, straightening, sharpening,' Camellia. You claim to do so well in that school. Don't they teach critical thinking? The rhubarb was just a red herring."

That was it. That was my last chance, and the witch was starting her incantation. "AH-beela AH-beelu, aBEElu, aBEElu . . ." she repeated. Blue smoke gathered in the pentagram. It coalesced from the chalk dust, rose up in the air, and filled an invisible pentagonal column with thick blue gas.

The scent of sulfur and rose petals filled the air. It grew very hot and my damp shirt clung to me. I sweated buckets, though the witch stayed dry as dust, her silver hair as crisp as ever. "Is this how it's supposed to go?"

"Progressing nicely!" shouted the witch. "Now watch this!"

She flicked her wand at the pentagram and a prism of glass shimmered into view, enclosing the pentagram and the blue gas. One more flick and the blue gas shot upward as if sucked into the ceiling by a vacuum cleaner.

When the gas cleared, there was the demon.

4

Boy-Band Boy

The demon was nine-feet high. He had orange horns circled by a brush of thick red hair. No, wait. They were green horns circled by a brush of thick blue hair. His skin was yellow, then it was turquoise, then it was baby blue. His size and shape didn't change, but all his colors did. It was like watching a living rainbow.

"Estahoth Elemental, Demon of the Fourth Layer, Second Earl of Kinetic Energy, do you agree that this is your correct and full address?" said the witch in a resonant voice.

"I do," said the demon in a voice like thunder.

"Then I propose to you the binding by which you may spend a short time on earth. One, I need a hundred pixies in Hal Headley High School on Friday, dead or alive. Two, I need precisely what this spell is asking for when it says, and I quote, 'the hopes and dreams of five.' Three . . ."

There was a taut silence, and then Sarmine continued. "You are no doubt familiar with the air elemental known as the phoenix, though you spend your time in the Earth's fiery core. As phoenix keep to the mountaintops, they have not been destroyed by humans as so many of the dragons were. Still, they live where we cannot reach them. Witches have named and numbered them over the centuries, tracking their hundred-year cycles. There were very few that lived at the altitude of this city."

"I am familiar with phoenix, yes," said Estahoth. "Do not

presume that you are the first witch to summon me. I am no virgin."

He leered at us, and despite the danger, the expression reminded me of someone imitating Elvis Presley. I clapped my hand to my mouth, choking down a burst of hysteria.

"Quite," said Sarmine. "Then you know how much power is contained in the phoenix's hundred-year death and birth."

"Atomic," the demon said simply.

"There is a phoenix known as R-AB1 which is due for its hundred-year explosion on this Halloween. This Friday evening at eight-forty. Indeed, Camellia and I settled in this town fifteen years ago to keep an eye on it. But fourteen years ago this phoenix disappeared."

"It could be anywhere in the world," scoffed the demon. "That's a needle in a haystack."

Sarmine raised a finger. "I have recently learned that when the phoenix disappeared, it was transfigured and hidden somewhere on the grounds of Hal Headley High School. You will find it by Friday, and then funnel the force of its magical explosion into my spell at my command."

"Pixies, hopes, and Phoenix Rabby," said the demon. "Check, check, check. Anything else?"

"Hold up," I said. "Just what do you mean by this 'hopes and dreams of five' stuff? And a *what*, a frikkin' atomic phoenix explosion at my school? What exactly is your plan here?"

The witch ignored me. Of course. I get no say in anything.

"Anything else?" repeated Estahoth.

"Well, since you asked so nicely—Moonfire's chest has been bothering her," I said. The witch glared at me, but I glared right back. "He's here, isn't he? And you said only an elemental could work magic on another elemental."

"I'm not glaring; this is my happy face. I'm pleased you're taking an interest," said the witch. Which of course made me bonkers because she knows perfectly well the only thing of *her* world I love is that dragon. "Estahoth, would you mind taking a look at the dragon's lungs?"

"Dragons, phoenix . . . nothing I'd rather do than play vet all day," said the demon. "Still, as long as I get my chance at embodiment I'll shake on it. Oh, I have such plans to rule your funny little world."

"I imagine," said the witch dryly. "Just don't think you'll get to fulfill any of those plans."

"Out of curiosity, why didn't you call the demon you called last time?" said Estahoth. "Nikorzeth's biggest hope in embodiment is to be another WitchNet star like Chadzeth."

"Because I need someone who can control a phoenix explosion," said Sarmine. "Such an opportunity comes rarely. I intend to combine one phoenix explosion plus the pixies plus the hopes plus many other secret ingredients to work the most powerful spell ever seen in this town. And to control this explosion will take not just an elemental, but a powerful elemental." The witch did not flatter or butter up, so I expected all this was nothing but the truth. "It takes someone more clever and powerful than Nikorzeth, poor fellow."

"Nikorzeth wouldn't know his own rear end if it were transformed into his elbow," Estahoth said. He smirked and it seemed like the demon and the witch shared a moment together, amused at the weakness of poor Nikorzeth. "Is that all?" Estahoth said.

"With one clause," said the witch. "Whether or not you complete my tasks, you will leave the instant the explosion of R-AB1 finishes. I'm aware that demons are bound by their own natural laws to *complete* contracts. But even if you fail at my tasks, you don't get to stick around." She drummed her fingers on her arm, considering. "That is all."

The demon puffed up, chest out, rainbows rippling. "Fantastic," he said. "Now do you want to hear my plan? My plan is to set up shop in the nice new body you give me and eat its soul." He pointed a sunshine-yellow claw at me. "That one looks young and healthy. Good choice. Once I achieve embodiment, I'll take over the world. Demon power here on earth, with no restrictions? I'll be unstoppable." He *mwa-ha-ha*'ed very impressively. "I'll outlaw all the witches so no demons can follow me. I'll control everything. How do you like my plan?"

"Hmph," I said. "I may not agree with her methods, but the witch will make you do as she says. I wouldn't *mwa-ha-ha* so fast if I were you. Right, Sarmine? Right?"

The demon smirked.

Sarmine shook her head. "No, Camellia. I cannot *compel* an elemental to do my bidding. What I can do is create an agreement we both bind ourselves to. If he wishes to spend time on earth, he will accept the obligation I wish him to fulfill. As demons think, quite incorrectly, that they are smarter than mortals, they always accept these agreements in hopes of stretching their contract long enough to achieve embodiment."

"Your souls are puny," growled Estahoth. "To let me roam around, you have to give me a body. Once I have a body, I can seduce that body's soul and then I am free. Free to live on Earth!" He roared the last line.

"Which is why I have procured you a mannequin," said the witch. Her heels clicked as she crossed to the pentagram. Her finger stabbed at the red-shirted figure slumped in the card table chair. "I have fed that mannequin one drop of dragon milk each day for the last twenty years," she said. "It has enough elemental magic to mimic a human body for three and a half days. That will be exactly enough time for you to complete the work I expect of you."

"This?" Estahoth peered down at the wide-eyed mannequin in the T-shirt. He poked her plastic shoulder. She tilted on the chair. "Are you as mad as a hatter? No. Can't be done."

The witch's dry lips cracked a thin smile. "I've done my research," she said. "In 1211, a demon named Hebroth was able to live on earth in an elemental-infused golem for one week. In that case, the golem was stuffed with phoenix feathers."

"Really?" said Estahoth.

"The demon might have been able to stay longer," said the witch, "except that, unfortunately, the mixture was not pure. There was a match mixed in with the phoenix feathers. As it jostled around, the feathers burst into flame and destroyed the golem. And, regrettably, the demon."

Estahoth's chest rippled red, purple red. He circled his pentagram prison, shimmering red hot. "Your kind does not call us so often anymore. I have been waiting to be released from the tormenting fire of the Earth's core. Waiting for my chance to *live*." His voice rose. He had great vocal support for someone with no diaphragm. "And now, you offer me this thing with no soul? Bah." He backhanded the mannequin and it smacked to the floor, bounced against the glass wall of the pentagram. "That is not playing the game fairly. I am deeply offended, Sarmine."

"Your offense bores me," said the witch. "You are contained in my pentagram, so you only have two choices. Accept my offer and have the mannequin for your earthly body. The goat's blood will bind you to it so you cannot leave it for a human body. Or, go home. Which is it, Estahoth?"

Estahoth put his arms out, as if testing the glass walls of the pentagram. Then the rainbow colors shimmered and his body dissolved. The rainbow lit up the glass like a prism for one gorgeous moment. Then with a *swoosh,* all the rainbow light went into the mannequin. It levered to its feet, awkwardly. Seemed to sniff the air. Sniff its fingers, like it was examining the spell that bound it. It pressed its stiff fingers against the glass.

"I accept," Estahoth said. The mannequin's lips did not move.

"Well chosen," said the witch. She touched her wand to the glass and inscribed a door.

The glass melted away and Estahoth stepped into our world. The rose/dragon/salamander smell dampened, replaced by a wet, moldy scent I last smelled when our basement flooded. Mold. Mold plus the sharp scent of firecrackers; that was the scent of this demon.

The demon-mannequin creaked around the basement, testing his limbs. The mannequin's cheekbones were chipped where she'd struck the floor, spots of white against the pink. Her painted eyelashes made her eyes seem wide with fear.

I swallowed. "Doesn't look very real," I said. "How do you think he's going to get around town looking like that?"

The mannequin swung around to look at me. It fixed me with painted black eyes.

Then it collapsed to the cement floor in a clattering pile.

The rainbow light rushed out of it and against me.

It was like standing in a tornado. The light had a force that beat against me like thunderous wind, battering me down with firecrackers and mold. I staggered, my back hit the wall, and then there was nowhere to go. "I thought . . . you said . . . goat's blood would contain him!" Instinctively I pushed against the rainbow light as hard as I could. The witch's demon was no way taking *me* over.

My eyes watered from the strain. My bones felt like they were being both squeezed and ripped apart at the same time. I pushed and pushed and pushed—

—and then suddenly, I tumbled forward onto the dusty basement floor as the demon withdrew, my hands smacking the cement. The rainbow light compressed, gathering force. "That wasn't goat's blood," he said in a pitch like struck crystal.

Then he rushed the witch.

This shows you how strong the witch is. She beat that tornado-force elemental back with the kind of glare she gives me for breaking the dried snakeskins.

The rainbow light filled the mannequin and it stood up. It wobbled on its jointed high-heeled feet, unsteady. If a mannequin needed to breathe, it would be breathing hard.

"Oh, please," said the witch. "You think we're not both well shielded? I'd just like to see a demon get into anybody with witch blood. Now tell me, Estahoth. What kind of blood was it?"

Stony silence.

"What kind?"

"Cow's," the demon said, and laughed sharply. "Not even strengthened with werewolf dung. I thought you knew bovines weren't good for anything but love potions and lucky charms."

The witch didn't spare the energy to look at me, but my jittery heart sunk to my tennis shoes regardless. Cow's blood! Had Kelvin always been giving me the wrong stuff, or was that his mom's doing?

The mannequin rocked back and forth. "You can't keep me away from humans forever."

"Yes, I can," said the witch calmly. "I have plenty of control over that plastic carapace." She pointed her wand at the demon. "Back in the pentagram you go. We will try this again tomorrow with real goat's blood."

The mannequin rocked toward the pentagram. I could tell that the witch, despite her calm words, was under a tremendous strain. Her left hand, hidden behind her back, was clenched and knotted as she tried to drive the demon back into the pentagram through sheer force of will. And so forceful was Sarmine's will that it seemed, almost, she was winning.

I held my breath, not daring to disturb even the air in the

basement as Sarmine pushed the mannequin toward the penta-gram.

And then the werewolf cub burst through the basement door and skidded down the steps, an entire bag of barbecued pig's ears swinging from his jaws. A blond boy thumped down after him. "Not all of them," he shouted. "I need those for Bingo! Heel, boy, heel!"

Wulfie ran smack under the mannequin's legs, jolting the demon out from what little control the witch had on him. Over they went in a pile, and the pig's ears flung from the bag, skit-tered across the cement floor.

Devon skidded to a halt and looked around in amazement at the scene in the basement. His eyes met mine. "Oh man," he said. "I didn't mean to come in, I mean, I was just chasing . . . I mean, your dog nearly took my thumb off grabbing that bag and—"

The rainbow light surged from the mannequin, bigger, wider, flashier. It grew and grew toward Devon.

"Devon! Run!" I shouted.

He tried to obey, but his foot slipped on the pile of pig's ears and he windmilled. Wulfie ran around his legs, howling.

The witch grabbed powders from her fanny pack, shouting the first part of a spell—

But we were all too late.

In a stream of rainbow light, the demon rushed out of the mannequin and into the boy collapsing in a pile of pig's ears.

5

Devon on the Loose

Devon stood up slowly. He looked around at us and then he grinned.

It was not any kind of bashful, blushing, boy-band-boy grin. It was pure malice.

It was very strange to see that ferocious look on Devon's kind face, and I have to admit that for a weird moment it made me realize how good-looking he was. He looked sure of himself, a boy that could do anything. Then I shook myself. This was no longer Devon.

This was Estahoth the demon in Devon's body.

And he was very, very powerful.

"Now Estahoth," said the witch crisply. "You get right back in that mannequin." She walked past me, wand out, and as she did she whispered fiercely, "See if he's still in there."

"Ha!" said Estahoth. "I like this body." He flipped up the collar on Devon's polo shirt like dorks do to look cool. Except, with the sneer in place . . . he almost *did* look cool. "I'm not going anywhere."

"Into the nice mannequin and we'll say no more about it," said the witch. "You don't want any trouble, do you?"

The witch sought my eyes and jerked her head at Devon's body. I swallowed. "Devon?" I said. "Devon, are you in there?"

"Hiding like a scared sprite," said Estahoth.

That made me mad. Devon might be a sweet boy with stage

fright, but any boy willing to dump water on a strange girl's fiery butt is a boy with strong character. I knew he wasn't cowering. He simply hadn't been invaded by a malevolent elemental before. He didn't know his options.

I imitated the witch's commanding tone. "Devon, come on out right now," I said. "The demon doesn't run your life. You can push your way out."

Devon's body kind of sagged. The arms jerked and the evil look on his face flickered on and off. Then it faded completely and the boy-band boy returned. "Cam?" he said. "Wh-what do I do?"

"We'll get him out," I said. "Won't we, Sarmine?"

"Of course," said Sarmine. "But you'll need to be brave for a while. Can you walk back to the pentagram?" If she could get Devon in the pentagram, she could seal it off. Of course, I didn't know what that would do to Devon, to be stuck in the pentagram with an angry demon. It sounded like a dangerous plan to me.

Devon took a ragged step, then another. It looked like he had invisible weights around his ankles.

Then the demon surged back up and ran with Devon in the other direction.

"Throw your shoe," shouted Sarmine.

"What?" But it's best to obey the witch, no matter how crazy she sounds. I yanked it off, not even untying the laces.

"At the demon! Do it!"

I beaned Devon in the head with my tennis shoe. He yelped and spun, feeling the back of his head. "Werewolf dung," the demon said slowly. "Strengthening the cow's blood, locking me into this body."

"It was a long shot," agreed the witch.

The demon sneered. "Never you mind. I like this body. It'll

be mine by Friday." He clattered through pig's ears and up the basement steps. "Suck it, witches!" he shouted, and then he was gone.

The basement was silent, except for the keening of Wulfie, who knew he'd effed up. The witch's shoulders slumped. My chest still hurt from the demon's attack.

"This is all your fault," I said to the witch. "What are you going to do?"

Nasty silence, and then the witch drew herself to a ramrod-straight position and glared down her nose at me. "I am not the one who supplied cow's blood," she said. "As punishment, you may start by cleaning up the basement."

"But—"

"As further punishment, mosquito bites," she said. She flicked her wand and itchy spots splattered my forearms like water droplets.

I shrieked and covered my arms. "But *Devon!*" I shouted, before she could think of more punishments. "You can't leave him like that. The demon will eat his soul."

The witch shrugged. "Not if Devon's strong enough. I once heard of a woman who lasted eight days. Estahoth is contractually bound to fulfill my agreements. When he's done, he has to go home. He can't break those rules."

Eight days could work. Devon only had to last three. "But what's typical?"

"One."

I scratched my arms. "I can't believe you," I said. "Causing all this chaos to find one lousy phoenix. Heaven knows what you're going to do with it."

"It's a brilliant spell," said the witch. "Everyone will remember having elected me as mayor last November. Manipulating minds takes a lot of power when you're talking one person. But when you're talking an entire city and a year's worth of history?

That takes more juice than the dragon could cry in a hundred years. They won't vote me in; very well, I'll vote myself in."

"That's not how democracy works," I said. I couldn't believe the whole reason the witch moved us here was because there was a phoenix at my high school. So much for choosing your town for a good school system. "Look, why would an air elemental want to live here when he could go home to his mountaintop? The dragon would be off in a minute if there were any others like her."

"The phoenix R-AB1 has always lived in this area, long before this city was built," said the witch. "It stayed here even after the roads went in and the buildings went up. Ninety years ago there was an enormous city fire. Those deluded humans said it was started by a cigarette, but we know the pattern, and it was phoenix fire. Several of us moved here in the last two decades. It was a good place to source phoenix feathers; you could always find a dropped one here or there if you knew how to look. I've been storing them.

"But fourteen years ago the phoenix disappeared. The witch community broke up somewhat after that; a lot of us moved on. It's been a bad century for witches. We keep to our tract houses, try to look normal. Witches all around the world are waiting for a rallying cry like mine, ready to bring us out of hiding." Sarmine's teeth bared. "Because I would do great things with this phoenix. Not like Kari."

"Kari?"

"She's the one who summoned a demon fourteen years ago and transfigured this phoenix so no one could find it. I had my suspicions, but recently my fears have been confirmed. She hopes to use the phoenix flame to her own disgusting ends, which I believe involve making herself very, very rich. This, I will not let her do. A phoenix flame is a powerful force, not to be used for something as déclassé as money."

"That's all well and good," I said. I picked up my shoe, which looked clean enough. I tried not to think about the werewolf poo molecules that were apparently lurking in its treads. "But you've now ruined this innocent boy. You have to help Devon."

The witch brushed dust and petal bits off her skirt. "If you wish to help your trespassing friend, then I suggest you help Estahoth carry out my demands," she said. "The quicker he's done here, the more chance your boy has." Her gaze raked the basement. "And don't skimp on the bleach."

☾

The blue chalk pentagram had adhered to the cement. It took three hours to scrub it clean, and then I still had to take dinner to the dragon. Moonfire ate an entire sheep twice a week, and the process consisted of hefting one from the big basement freezers and setting it out to defrost, then taking the already defrosted one and slow-roasting it in the basement oven for twelve hours while I was at school. (Sure, lots of apex predators eat their meat raw. Not dragons.)

But I loved Moonfire. I hefted the sheep in its battered roasting pan up the basement steps and out the back door to the RV garage. Moonfire rumbled inquisitively at me as I backed through the door with my pan full of sheep.

Moonfire is hard to see. Like all female dragons, she's part blue, part translucent, and part invisible. Trying to see her is a little like looking at one of those old-timey Magic Eye pictures. If you figure out how to focus, then suddenly the little blue bits and the translucent bits and the way that things are slightly warped when viewed through the invisible bits combine to make a dragon. I had painted the garage sky blue long ago to give her extra protection in case someone ever peered in to see why the garage had a smoking chimney. I'm used to her, though, and when you're used to something it's more obvious.

I plopped the warm sheep in front of her. Moonfire nuzzled my hand in thanks and I skritched her scales. She was definitely my favorite member of the household. I sunk to the painted concrete, leaned back against her warm side, and stretched out my legs till they met the garage wall. My still-damp tennis shoes were tufted with straw and dust bunnies, and they wafted bleach back to my nose.

I'd forgotten *The Crucible* to read to her, so I told her a story I'd told her over and over since I was little.

"Once upon a time," I said, "there were a mommy and daddy who were very excited to have a baby. An innocent little baby, who would soon have blue eyes and a smooshed nose that everyone says *someday* she'll grow into, though she's wondering how much *someday* is left, since she's already fifteen.

"Anyway. There was one thing the mommy wanted, and that was chocolate pickles. So the daddy went out to find them. He tried the corner mart, he tried the twenty-four-hour drugstore. And just when he was about to buy pickles from the deli and dip them in melted candy bars, a long-nosed old woman appeared out of nowhere and offered him a whole container of chocolate-covered pickles in exchange for cash. Proud of himself, he ran home to his wife, beamed with fatherly pride, and said: 'You know, it was the strangest thing. She said she'd take cash, but she said she'd come for it later.'"

I rubbed Moonfire's scales hard with the scale brush she likes. She coughed bits of roasted sheep at me, then purred.

"Four months later the mommy had a baby girl, with nutmeg hair and blue eyes. And in the tired haze she named it Camellia after her mother and Anna after his mother and Stella because she wanted her little girl to be a star.

"And when an ugly old woman picked Camellia Anna Stella Hendrix out of the baby room and took her away forever and ever? Well, nobody lived happily ever after. The end."

The dragon purred some more and rolled so I could reach her belly. Dragons don't talk, but they're not animals. They're elementals, and all three elementals are smart, even if the dragons don't communicate in the same way humans do. If you get close to dragons you can pick up their emotional vibrations, and sometimes even pictures. It's usually nostalgia for the old days mixed with *I miss my dragon sisters*, but when I'm there, she sends me extra thrums of comfort, almost like I'm her kit.

I stroked the dragon's neck, then flicked messy bits of sheep back into the roasting pan. "Think to me of the old days," I said, warm against her hide. "Think to me what you miss."

The dragon's pictures are like dreams. The more you try to focus on them, the quicker they fade. This story was the one she'd told me the most, so I'd pieced it together over all our years together. I saw it more clearly because I could practically tell it to myself.

She showed me an old world, a world with no paved roads, no buildings, no radar to mark the passage of unidentified flying dragons. Hills and hills of rolling green and gold, and here and there the passage of people, the smoke of campfires. She soared high, with a daughter behind her, and their sky-blue bellies reflected light. Their translucent limbs disappeared in the atmosphere. From below, they looked like bits of glittering sky, invisible unless you knew how to look. They landed in the plains and ate buffalo; they landed in the mountains and ate nuggets of gold. Male dragons were uncamouflaged. They were bright: reds and oranges. They fought each other, and then there was flame, and forest fires.

"Why can't female dragons spit fire?" I said. "Doesn't that make you mad?"

She thought of a male dragon, searing a female who would not mate. She thought of herself and her sisters, surrounding him, tearing him to bits. She thought of more and more male dragons dying in their own wars, until they had all gone. She thought of her sisters, caught and destroyed one by one by men in green and brown, all over the world. She used to think she caught a wavelength, a rumble of *Draconis* late at night . . . but even this had faded in recent years. Hard to know if they were all truly gone, or merely impossible to hear in the modern crush of sound and radio waves.

Dragon milk welled in her eyes and dripped into the glass jam jars that hung around her head to catch the excretions. Her neck sagged and she coughed, her wheeze shaking the jam jars against her side with *clink-clinks*. "We'll get your chest looked at, I promise," I said. I leaned my head into her rough scales and sent back images of one of my plane trips. I'd been sent to Brazil at thirteen to courier ingredients home for the witch. I showed her our plane flying through gold-lit clouds, I showed her tops of textured green trees, and I felt her warm rumble of enjoyment beneath me.

Spending time with her almost made up for the fact that when I finally made it inside, I found that the werewolf pup had been so upset with himself for his part in the demon disaster that he'd chewed up my feather pillow and my left toe-loop sandal. Then hid under the bed, his tail wagging the dust ruffle like mad. Short tufts of werewolf hair floated out, silver in the lamplight.

"Come on out, Wulfie," I said. "It wasn't really your fault." He whined and licked my fingers, but he couldn't talk in this state. (I dunno about all werewolves, but ours is only human on the full moon. He's three years old, so once a month is plenty, believe me.) "Tomorrow's another day," I said. I dumped my jeans on the floor and my cell phone fell to the carpet.

I stuffed my featherless pillow with an old sweatshirt and tossed it and the phone on the bed. The phone landed on a printout the witch had left for me. After punishments, she frequently left directions for an antidote spell in my room. Of course, since I couldn't work the darn things, it was basically further punishment just to see them.

The anti-itching spell on the printout started, "Take pi slices of blueberry pie . . ."

I flicked it to the floor, scratching my arms. "I don't do spells," I muttered.

I put the makeshift pillow behind me and picked up my phone. The phone was still black and cold, and I hadn't brought up any dragon milk.

I swallowed. "I don't *do* spells," I repeated. The window cleaner I spritz on for the bus driver, the disinfectant I'd flicked on the ninth grader—that magic came from the original animal or elemental. It worked regardless of who did the sprinkling.

Not so with real spells.

They required thought, patience. Intention.

Witch blood.

"And I am *not* a witch, no matter what she says." Wulfie licked my foot.

Still, elementals were powerful, even if I wasn't a witch myself. Perhaps the dragon on my skin would be enough to boost my phone up again. I rubbed my dragon-smelling fingers around the keypad. "Up we go," I said, like the phone was Wulfie. "Up we go." Then I pressed the "power" button one more time.

This time it came up.

"Maybe it wasn't really dead," I told Wulfie. He settled in on my feet and draped his head across my ankles.

Back to my demon bookmark. Ah, there it was: "The best way to stop a demon is not to summon it."

Too late for that.

"Demons are bound by their contracts," it continued. "Even the smartest witches have difficulty demonproofing the terms of their contracts. Demons are on the alert for any loopholes. A demon bound to a contract is obligated to continue working on it, and the only way to banish a demon is to fulfill the contract. Even this can lead to difficulties, such as in the case of Jim Hexar in 1982, when such a contract effectively prevented any chance of him winning his Head Warlock bid."

Hexar, I thought. Was that the same Hexar as the Hexar/Scarabouche T-shirt the mannequin wore? I had no idea the witch had had real political aspirations once. All the attempts at city-running I'd seen involved spells and schemes, not rallies and debates. I suppose I'd thought the shirt was a joke. It was hard to imagine Sarmine as a T-shirted young rebel in 1982, knowing her as the ancient-looking support-hosed witch I knew now.

Though if she still acted like a twenty-year-old, it would be a lot easier to imagine it—because she'd look like it.

See, witches live a long time, often three times as long as humans. But the interesting thing about witches is that they look whatever age they feel like inside. I don't mean they can choose, exactly, though they sort of do. Basically they look the age they feel . . . and most of them feel old, which is why one of the things regular humans get right is imagining that all witches are ancient humpbacked crones.

Because . . . yeah. I think all that paranoia gets to you, that and feeling a million times smarter than all the humans around you. Witches aren't as a rule any smarter, as any trip around the WitchNet will show you, but they know magic, and they know they're going to live a long time. If you know you're going to be around to see it, you look at the fate of the world differently.

Not that that gave Sarmine Scarabouche the right to wreak havoc on my high school.

I clicked on "Jim Hexar," but the biography was terse:

"Vanished near the beginning of the twenty-first century," it said, and then there was a smoky-smelling sign that said the article had been flagged for having virus spells attached to it. I shut off my phone before one could sneak through.

Fulfill the contract, I thought. I turned off the light and smooshed my sweatshirt pillow into a better position. So Estahoth/Devon was going to be busy working on Sarmine's contractual list of world-taking-over duties. If Witchipedia was right, there was no way to send a demon back to the Earth's core until its contract was up. But what about getting a demon out of a particular human? Did such a demon-getting-out spell even exist?

Well, even if it did, the witch wasn't going to work it for me. I dismissed that option from my mind. It seemed like my best bet to save Devon's soul was to help him complete the contract so the demon would leave.

Which apparently included destroying five people and maybe making the school burn down.

Un dilemme, indeed.

6

Sparkle This

Devon was not on the bus the next morning. I walked up and down the aisle, checking, even though Oliver the bus driver looked at me funny and made a crack about walking to school.

He was also not in Algebra II, which made me more nervous. Was the demon *that* in control of him that he couldn't make it to school? I didn't even know where he lived. What if the demon had already eaten his soul?

At lunch, Jenah stopped me at the cafeteria door. "There's catering where we're going," she said.

"Where are we going?" I said.

Jenah made shifty eyes. "You remember how you said you owed me big-time for tracking down Kelvin yesterday?"

"And I stand by that," I said. "Wait, you aren't going to ask me to clean your half of the locker again, are you? It's like a fake-hair factory exploded down there, and it's only October."

"It's nothing bad," Jenah said quickly.

"Good," I said, as we set off down the hall. "And this nothing bad thing is . . . ?"

"Very last Halloween Dance Committee meeting," Jenah said in a fast mumble. Like *very last* made it better.

I stopped. "Jenah, you know I hate Halloween."

She grabbed my hand. "Yes, but you promised. Come on."

"I don't know why you need me," I said. Jenah understood dances. Parties. Committees. Today she was all in black and yellow, stripes and fishnets. Her clipped-in streak was high-lighter yellow, and her eyes were winged in perfect cat's-eye liner. I was in my second-best jeans—the ones that didn't understand my butt and showed too much sock—and a vintage tee with a glittery rainbow.

It was obvious who should be on the HDC.

"The aura in that room is just awful," said Jenah. "I need you to balance it out with me. You know what they can be like."

They? "Jenah," I said, "is Sparkle on the committee?"

Jenah grimaced. "Trying to run things, as usual." The only person I've ever seen cow Jenah is Sparkle. Sparkle can make you feel more ridiculous than an elephant trying to squeeze into a tutu.

"I'll run backup." I sighed. "The way I feel today, Sparkle just better not say anything."

"How *do* you feel?" said Jenah. "You look green and jittery around the edges. Rosemarie said she saw you on the bus with the new boy yesterday afternoon. He seems a little . . . off in his own world, doesn't he? Always with those earbuds?"

"There's a reason for that," I said defensively. I couldn't tell Jenah the demon story, so I doled out other gossip. "Did you know he's in a band?"

"Ooh!"

"He's supposed to sing lead on the songs he writes, but he's still working on his stage fright. He's really very sweet. And kind." *And he has a lovely velvety voice . . .*

"We could help him with his stage fright," said Jenah. "I just knew our lines were bound to be entangled in some way. I could see it from the moment I saw him."

"You and me both," I muttered.

"No cryptic utterances," Jenah said firmly, "Or else—"

"Our galactic jump rope gets in a knot. I know. You don't really need me for Sparkle, do you?"

Jenah suddenly stopped. "Ooh, isn't that him? What on earth happened?"

A tall, weary boy was slodging through the crowds milling around the front door.

It was the weirdest thing, but when I looked at him the first time, it looked as though his hair was completely black.

But it must've been the way the shadows and backpacks moved, because when he looked up and saw us, he was his normal blond boy-band self, except very, very tired-looking.

His face cleared at the sight of me. "Cam," he said, and then stopped. He blinked and swayed on his feet, like he was too tired to think of words after that. His jeans were muddy and his T-shirt sleeve was torn. He was carrying a cardboard box, also muddy, with little bits of stalks and grass stuck into the mud. A leggy lump on the top looked like a squished water bug.

"What happened to you?" I said.

For an answer, he lifted the flap of the box about a half inch. I peered in, and through the light from the airholes punched in the top, I saw a hoppy mass. For a moment I thought they were frogs, but then I saw that the little green blobs had wings. Sparkly green wings that winked in and out of sight like lightning bug bellies.

Pixies.

"Wow," I said. "One hundred?"

"One hundred," said Devon.

"One hundred . . . ?" said Jenah.

"Frogs," I lied. "One hundred frogs."

Devon nodded to Jenah over the box and lifted dirty fingers. "I'm Devon," he said. "I'm new."

"True but not very explanatory," she said. "I'm Jenah; I'm in your algebra *and* your American history, so I already know some-things about you but not the most important question: *Why* do you have a box of frogs?"

"Science project," I said.

Jenah looked thoughtful. "None of the science classes are currently doing projects."

"Extra credit?" suggested Devon.

"Catching up from his old school," I said simultaneously.

Jenah shook her head at us, lips pursed like she was buying none of it. She pointed a finger at me. "Thirty seconds," she said, and then collared a passing Mohawked boy to catch up on the latest news from the punk world.

Devon smiled shyly at me.

"How are you, um, doing with you-know-who?" I said.

"I tried to go to sleep last night but he dragged me down to the creek behind my house," he said. "We caught four pix—er, frogs there. Then down the creek to where it goes in the sewer pipe. Another two frogs inside the sewer. Then he marched my legs overland till we found where the creek starts up again. Like, half a mile. Another three frogs. The creek widened until it hit a lake. All around the lake were enormous houses with motion detectors that went off if I chased the frogs in the wrong direc-tion. By then it was after midnight . . ."

"Gah," I said.

"I just found number one hundred in a culvert three miles from here," he said. "I found a bus stop, but the driver wouldn't let me on with a box of pix—frogs. I don't mean to complain." He yawned. "I'm just dead."

"What's he doing now?" I said. "You know. *Him.*"

"Catching up on sleep," Devon said in a low voice. "And now I have to figure out how to save these frogs. I had to fight to put airholes in the box, and a bowl of water. His reflexes are better than mine, so I tried to encourage him to catch some flies for the box. I don't even know if they eat flies."

I nodded. "Flies, spiders, and dew that still has dawn reflected in it."

"I couldn't see them at first till he rubbed my eyes around with his fingers," said Devon. "*My* fingers. Whatever. Now my eyes feel like they're full of Vaseline." He shrugged his shoulders, swaying again. "I could crumble up an energy bar for the frogs. Do you think they'd eat it?"

"Doubtful," I said. Pixies were picky. "I could help you catch spiders after school if you want. But they definitely need the dew tomorrow at dawn or their lights will dim."

"I remember the first time I dealt with a kitten at the shelter that wouldn't eat anything," Devon said. "Tried cloth soaked in milk, baby formula, water . . . Dunno why I didn't think of dawn-reflected dew."

"Ready to go?" said Jenah from across the hall.

Devon bent toward me. "How can I deal with it, Cam?" he said urgently. "Estahoth said he's here till Friday no matter what. How can I make it two more days without going crazy? Everything he made me do last night, from smashing birds' nests to throwing the pixies in the box with no food . . . He's my opposite. What do I do?"

Little blows shook my soul. How could I explain to him how his words hit home? How do you deal when some random statement hits to the core of your deepest fears?

We looked at each other for ages. I don't think either of us could've spoken if we tried.

Then Jenah grabbed my arm and the moment collapsed. "Have. To. Go," she said. "Come on down to the choir room if you get a chance, Devon. I've got ideas for you." She grinned and dragged me down the crowded hallway. "Mick says the punks poll one hundred percent in favor of Lice Blanket, and zero percent in favor of the band Sparkle wants. God, the only people who like that band are Sparkle's girls and maybe also the pink-sweater-vest crowd."

"You don't have to pull," I finally managed, halfway down the hall.

"Oh good, Miss Giant," she said. "Then come on."

"If you were any shorter, I'd step on you," I said. I went through the motions of the familiar teasing, but I was still thinking about someone driving my life, someone who was the opposite of everything I stood for.

But we were at the door to the choir room. "Focus! Free food!" Jenah said in my ear, and shoved me through.

The room was full of Sparkle's friends, claiming the space by draping themselves on the risers and around the piano. Jenah was right: deep soul-searching would have to wait. I shook my head and tried to focus.

The catering was good as usual when Sparkle was involved. No, I don't know why we get catering for a party-planning committee, except that Sparkle gets her best friend Reese's mom to donate for whatever Sparkle wants. I'm not complaining. Sushi and sashimi out the ears, plenty of the stuff I like and the witch hates. I get to eat Cantonese at Jenah's place (her mom sighs and fixes it when the tradition-loving grandparents are there), and pizza when I sneak off by myself on teacher workday holidays (I don't tell the witch those days exist), but otherwise it's beet salad and raw carrots all the way. The witch refuses to get take-out because she says the delivery people's vibes interfere with her spells or something.

Sparkle was standing by the spider rolls in a white tank and turquoise sequined skirt. I could almost feel cheery toward Sparkle for the catering choices, but of course she immediately studied my butt in my second-best jeans and said, "You should definitely have some more tempura, Camellia."

I put another handful of fried things on my plate. "Excellent suggestion," I said. "You should definitely have some more total pain in the—"

"Oh, Camellia, don't," said Miss Crane ineffectually. We all knew Miss Crane, as she was the choir teacher, and also the one dumped with unfun tasks like trying to stop Sparkle from running everything. She was probably young, but she wore long shapeless skirts and button-down shirts like a refugee from one of her own choir concerts. "Grab your food and sit down, girls. This is our last chance to finalize." She perched on the edge of her high stool as if she would flee at any moment.

"Something's going down," Jenah whispered to me. "I can feel it." She whisked over to a random girl, not one of Sparkle's, and moved her to the top riser. "You sit here," she said to the girl. "Better feng shui." Jenah moved the trash can next to Sparkle's sidekick Reese and sat down again.

"Jenah, please," said Miss Crane. "The party is this Friday and I need to double check the last few party essentials. Benjamin, do you have the receipts for the streamers? And, Sparkle, I *still* need to approve the playlist for the band."

"I've approved it," said Sparkle from her spider-roll position.

Miss Crane fluttered her hands, her hot-pink manicure flashing arcs through the air. The manicure always made me wonder if she had a secret life in which she wore non-choral clothes and didn't let teenage girls walk all over her. "I know you have excellent taste, Sparkle, but, er, per the school board, I have to approve what's in their songs, or they can't play."

"Pop Pop is all set," said Sparkle. "End of discussion."

"Pop Pop?" said Jenah. "We settled on Lice Blanket and you know it."

"I don't think a band called Lice Blanket would be ideal," protested Miss Crane. "I'm positive their lyrics would never make it past the school board. Now, Sparkle. What kind of music does Pop Pop play?"

Sparkle rolled her eyes at the ceiling. "You should definitely invite whatever band you want, Jenah," she said. "The Halloween Dance would be remembered for all time."

"Oh, good, an agreement," said Miss Crane. "Now if I can just—"

"Excellent," said Jenah to Sparkle's sarcasm. She snapped her fingers at me. "What's that new band we were just listening to, Cam? So new we were totally ahead of the curve."

"Huh?" I said.

"You know," said Jenah. "It has that green-eyed boy in it. The new kid. What's his name, Dev, Dannon, what?"

"Oh," I said, catching on. "Blue Crush. They're sensational. Really, er, fresh. But, uh, I don't know if they're available to play." I was torn—Jenah's idea would be an awesome way for poor Devon to practice getting over his stage fright, and of course I would love to hear him sing . . . but on the other hand, I had to get that demon out of him, and the fewer distractions, the better.

On the *other* other hand, Pop Pop stunk.

"I'm confused," said Sparkle's sidekick, Reese. "Sparkle's band is set. Why would we be changing it now? That's not cool." Her brown eyes crinkled in befuddlement.

"You'd know what's not cool," I said innocently.

"True," Reese said, nodding. "Besides, have you seen how hot the boy in Pop Pop is? Oh. My. God." This was met with squeals of agreement from the Sparkle supporters on the risers.

Sparkle glared at us. "Reese's mother is paying for the band, and she's paying for Pop Pop."

"So, the playlist for Pop Pop," said Miss Crane. "Can they email me their lyrics so I can check for improper allusions?" She peered at Sparkle. "Do you think they'll have email?"

"What's Blue Crush?" said Benjamin, raising his hand. "Are they a surfer band? We've never had a surfer band."

"They're an everything band," said Jenah. She leaned back on the risers. "Surfers will like them. Ravers will like them." She looked at Reese. "The lead singer's really cute, so Pop Pop lovers will like them. And as soon as we book them, Devon can give us the lyrics immediately."

"Oh, that would give me time to read them," said Miss Crane. "Maybe he can send them to me from the computer lab. Do you think he has a file of their lyrics at school? Like on his phone, is that a thing?"

"My mom would totally approve of supporting a band with a hot boy from the school," said Reese.

"Excellent!" said Jenah. "We're all set, then."

"We are *not* all set," growled Sparkle.

"Oh, the disco ball wants to talk," I said.

"You just watch yourself, Cash," said Sparkle. "Little Miss My-Mother's-an-Evil—"

I had my last tempura shrimp ready to throw at her stupid sparkle lip gloss when Reese's dim-witted squeal interrupted her. "Ohmigod, who's that?"

We all turned.

Standing in the doorway was a punk-band boy.

7

Punk~Band Boy

There was a gaga moment where I didn't recognize him. For one, this boy had black hair, not blond. For two, I'd just seen him ten minutes ago torn and muddy, carrying a box of froggy-looking pixies. The Devon I knew was nothing like this boy here.

This boy had style.

This boy had cool.

This boy was looking down Sparkle's shirt.

"Devon!" I said. I grabbed his sleeve (now not torn). "How are you feeling?"

He tossed back his ink-black hair and looked amused. I felt six years old. "Hey, Flower Girl," he said. "Come to get a piece of the action?"

"Ew," I said, but all the same I thought I might be blushing. I peered into his green eyes, searching for any trace of Devon there. Surely this wasn't Devon . . . but what if Estahoth was already getting to him? Already warping his mind, making him think disgusting inhuman thoughts . . . ?

He looked back into my eyes, completely unself-conscious and with a smirk in his (now) black eyebrows. A sharp smell of firecrackers curled around him, underlaid with the musty tang of mold. The way he looked at me was like he knew me . . . inside and out. I suddenly remembered that the demon had actually been inside me for a few seconds in the basement. Then I really did blush, red hot.

I tossed back my hair and tried to regain my normal cool. I mean, I've had a couple boyfriends. Plenty of guy friends. When your life revolves around filling the outrageous demands of a cranky witch, other social interactions seem way less scary. Okay, maybe I wasn't made of cool like Jenah, and maybe boys didn't just drop dead at my feet like they did for Sparkle, but in general, boys were not foreign scary creatures. Not compared to two-hundred-year-old warlocks who might give you appendicitis just for *asking* them if they'd barter three unicorn hairs for a drop of dragon milk (true story).

So. There was no way *any* boy was going to get the best of me, no matter how much he suddenly resembled my TV love, Zolak the demon hunter. "Um, this is Devon," I managed. "With Blue Crush."

Reese squealed, and suddenly she and the rest of the girls in the room were sucked into Devon like he was pure gravity. The risers clattered as the girls leaped on him. "Oh my god, we are *so* booking you to play for us!" said Reese. "You are way hotter than that boy from Pop Pop."

"Play for you?" said Devon. He did a thing that was like a wink, but it was way cooler than a wink. "You mean . . . personally?"

Reese looked like she was about to faint.

"Um, maybe we should just stick with Pop Pop," I said. This new Devon did not need anybody's help with stage fright. It was weird, but it was like the demon inside him gave him an extra allure. Like he could sing "Head, Shoulders, Knees and Toes" and all the girls in the room would swoon.

And if a billion girls swooned on him he'd never get the witch's tasks completed.

And then Devon's soul would be eaten.

"You're very busy, right?" I said meaningfully at Devon. "Extra-credit science projects to finish?"

His green eyes fixed me again but this time I managed not to blush. After all, this was not regular Devon. There was a million-year-old elemental in there, warping Devon's thoughts. "I'm never too busy for my music," he said. "What's the gig?"

I glared back and refused to think about how hot he was with the dark hair and the sudden confidence. "Halloween Dance. You're too busy. You've got *ob-li-ga-tions*."

Despite all the girls clinging to Devon, I noticed that Sparkle was standing apart from him like I was. Her arms were crossed over her chest, she was clutching her cameo, and she was looking at Devon in a very weird way. I couldn't tell if it was confusion—or fear. Both seemed like weird emotions for Sparkle to have about a cute new boy. She couldn't be picking up on his internal demon somehow . . . could she?

"You're probably too busy adjusting to your new school," Sparkle said. "Besides, we've already booked a band, I'm afraid. Miss Crane is prepared to approve their lyrics."

"*Prepared* to," said Miss Crane. Her fingers gripped the edge of the piano lid, her voice quavering as she tried for *firm*. "But first I *need* them, or we'll have no band at all."

"Lyrics?" said Devon. "I wrote our lyrics. I could recite them right here."

Reese glanced at Sparkle. "Well . . . Couldn't we . . . ?"

"*Reese*," said Sparkle. There was a tone in her voice that usually Reese would've obeyed instantly.

But mortal junior Sparkle versus the magnetism of an immortal elemental force?

Reese stared up at Devon, who winked/not winked at her again. "I'm unbooking them," she said dreamily but firmly. "Pop Pop isn't even part of the school. We're supporting the new boy's band."

Devon grinned lazily. "Can't wait to perform for y'all."

Reese sighed moistly and the other girls squealed. Miss

Crane beamed and moved in for those lyrics. Even Benjamin joined the admiring mob.

I groaned, grabbed one more spider roll, and snuck out of the room. Left the squealing behind me.

What on earth was I going to do now? Devon was supposed to complete three tasks—none of which I was sure he *should* complete—so we could get the demon out before it ate his entire soul and owned Devon forever. The sooner we could get the tasks done, the sooner the demon would be gone—and every minute might count.

But maybe the newly confident Devon wouldn't *want* the demon out of his soul. A demon could make a boy with stage fright into a star.

That was a nasty thought.

There was a tug on my backpack and it turned out to be Jenah. "Okay, that A Lunch was full of win," she said. "Did you see Sparkle's face when Reese disobeyed her? Hey, so what do you think about the nose job rumors with Sparkle? It definitely looks different, but everyone knows it's just her living with her grandfather or something, and god knows what he does, but it no way involves piles of cash and anyway, what kind of doctor would perform a nose job at her age? That's a mystery, I tell you." Jenah with the auras straightened out was giddy with relief.

But me, I felt like a ton of bricks. Maybe it was my backpack. At least, something was weighing me down.

"Okay, spill what's wrong," said Jenah. "I'm trying to cheer you up, but something's wrong and I'm betting some part of it has to do with Devon. And no, I don't know how he changed his hair that fast, but I expect there's a sink in a boys' bathroom covered in black dye. Look, you're not even thrilled about getting rid of that awful Pop Pop. Hey, over here. Talking, talking, me."

We stopped at our locker and I thumped my backpack to the ground. I didn't feel any lighter. I traded out my books for the American history text and Jenah grabbed a lime-green hair streak and clipped it next to the highlighter-yellow one.

"You're always trying to help people out," Jenah said. "And you like Devon. Why'd you suddenly change your mind about helping him?"

"Does he look like he needs our help?" I said.

"No," admitted Jenah. "His aura sure was different. All purple-black." She watched me stare into the hairy depths of the locker. "Cam," she said. "What's wrong?"

A billion things welled up inside me but I couldn't say any of them, because they all traced back to the witch in my life.

Devon's demon.

The destruction of the school.

The dragon's loneliness.

"I don't want to buy pig's ears ever again," is what finally came out.

"Okaaay," Jenah said. She studied the air around me, like she did when she was looking at her invisible auras.

I could never figure out if she really saw anything. But again, who was I to judge? My frustration swirled around in my brain.

Jenah touched a finger to an invisible spot next to my shoulder, then shook her head. "Way too mustardy," she said. "You and I. Need to cut class. You will tell me about the pig's ears and the box of frogs."

"Don't be ridiculous," I said, brushing her finger aside. "I can't cut American history and you can't cut English. You *like* English."

"That's why I can cut it," said Jenah. "But fine. We'll meet after school. You've got something you need to share and I'm here for you."

The thought of sharing the awfulness that was the witch

made my stomach churn. "I've got stupid algebra tutoring after school," I said. I slung my backpack over my shoulders and turned. I tried to laugh off Jenah's concern, but the words came out bitter and obviously false. "Anyway, there's nothing to share."

I strode off to American history and I didn't look back.

As always, American history was full of cheesy videos (I could've cut, I know), AP biology was fascinating, and gym was sweaty. Biology's my all-time fave, so it trumped my worries about Devon and his pixie-frogs for an hour. But when we started running boring hurdles around the track in gym, it all came pouring back.

Possibly it also didn't help that Reese is in my hour of gym and she kept bringing girls up to me and telling me to tell them how cute Devon was.

It's obvious that the only reason Reese is popular is because she's Sparkle's best friend, and not to be catty, but I'm pretty sure the reason Sparkle's best friends with a dingy sophomore like Reese is because she's rich and Sparkle isn't. Reese herself is nice to everyone because it's easy to be. She doesn't pick fights or humiliate girls just for fun. Sure, this makes her mostly harmless and fools a lot of people. But put a girl like Reese who's nice because it's convenient next to someone like Celeste at the grocery store who actually believes in doing good for people, and you'll see the difference. I'm not saying Reese was nice to purposely cover up a big malicious black-hearted void, although I've known girls like that. I'm saying she was a dim bulb who gave no thought to moral right and wrong, and whose superficial manners happened to be pleasant. I wouldn't trust her farther than I could throw her.

Reese's backbone today against her leader, Sparkle, was an unusual event, which is why I suspected it was demon inspired.

Because the rule of thumb here at Triple H is this: whatever Sparkle says, is so.

I told three girls on the hurdles that yes, Devon had green eyes, two girls in the shower that yes, Devon had floppy black hair, and one extra-persistent girl that no, I did not know his email, or his shampoo type, or whether or not he would like gifts of soda and cheese whirls left next to his locker.

By the time I got to the algebra classroom I was Devoned out. It was a relief to see someone sitting in Rourke's room who was guaranteed not to ask me about Devon.

"Kelvin? Are you waiting for the tutor, too?"

"Kelvin is the tutor," Kelvin said in his robot voice.

"Very funny. But I'm on to your sense of humor."

"I am," he said normally. His black sleeves were rolled partway up, revealing a retro plastic watch. "Is it just chapter three you need help with, or do we need to go back farther than that?"

"No, just chapter three," I said. "I understand the other stuff from Algebra One. I had Mrs. O'Malley for that and it went A-OK." I dropped my backpack on a desk, smelling the familiar math classroom scents of dry-erase dust and root beer. I parked my butt on the skinny pink back of a chair, where I could see the hallway through the open door over Kelvin's shoulder. I was still confused. "Rourke said the tutor was sick yesterday—but I saw you after school."

Kelvin looked behind him to see if Visible Undershirt was still in the room. "If I'd known it was you, I wouldn't have told him I was going home early." He looked flustered for a moment and I didn't know why. "You remember you needed me to meet you at the Thunderbird with goat's blood?"

"Of course," I said, and then the rest of those events hit me. "Wait a minute. Wait one frikkin' minute." I stood up from the chair back. "That wasn't goat's blood."

"Yes, it was. I always get you goat's blood." Robot voice: "Kelvin rotate through goats."

Shudder. "No. This time it wasn't. Are you sure you told your mom goat's? Because it was cow's blood. It messed up my . . . experiment."

He looked shifty.

"Kelvin?"

Kelvin lifted his chin and stared me in the eye. "Sorry, Cam," he said. "We don't even keep cows. It was definitely goat's."

I sighed. "All right, I believe you." I dug my wallet from my backpack and handed over the remainder of the cash I owed him. "Something sure got screwed up, though."

Kelvin tucked the bills into some pocket deep in his backpack. From its recesses he said, "So, algebra. You should get this because you're good at science. You've got a logical mind."

"I used to think math was logical, but this year it seems like you just have to be born understanding it." I stared glumly around the room at the posters of geometric figures and Escher staircases. "Wait, how did you know I like science? You're not in biology with me."

"Your science fair projects in grade school," Kelvin said, stowing his backpack under the seat. He emerged with a perfectly sharpened pencil, which he pointed at me. "You beat me one year with your project about the theoretical genetics of werewolves. Pounded my ego flat as a pancake. I had nightmares about being attacked by your blue ribbon."

"I did?" I felt bad for not remembering that Kelvin participated, too. Was I supposed to know that? I hadn't paid much attention to the other projects. If I'd managed to get something done at all, between all my regular chores, I counted it a win. Besides, I rarely made it to the actual fair, because I was so busy making sure the witch didn't go.

"Is that what the goat's blood is for this year?" he said.

"'Because that's gotta be an interesting project. Maybe you could give me a behind-the-scenes tour. Show me all the blood and guts, so to speak." Then deadpan added, "No, literally."

"Er, no," I said. "I don't have time for the fair this year. I have to concentrate on figuring out this math."

"Input received," Kelvin said, and it sounded like it should have been in a robot voice, but it wasn't. He looked away from me, down at the textbook. Shrugged his trench coat off and back on his shoulders. "Let's start with basic algebraic multiplication and build from there. The problem with Rourke's teaching is that he shows you the steps once and then he expects you to just do them in your head from there on out. So, basics. Show me how you multiply $2(x+5)$."

"Okay, I think that's $2x+10$," I said. "Right? It's just when we get into word problems that I get lost. They have all this misleading stuff and you have to sort through it and . . . it's like Rourke expects you to just see where his answer came from. He just naturally understands it, I guess, and I don't."

"You will," said Kelvin, "if we do it our way, which is one step at a time. No leaps necessary. If you can do $2(x+5)$, you can do it all." He grabbed the study guide for the test I'd bombed and worked through the first problem with me (some gawdaw-ful thing about sides of triangles totaling sides of rectangles), one piece at a time.

First we wrote down what we knew. We crossed out what we didn't need. It almost made sense when I took each step slowly instead of trying to leap to the end like Rourke did. We got through three whole problems before Mr. Visible Under-shirt himself came in.

Slouching behind him was Devon.

Devon with the demon-black hair.

I wondered idly how the demon had known that black would

look totally hot on Devon. Estahoth must have learned something in his previous trips to Earth.

"You've got two months of work to catch up on," said Mr. Rourke in a low voice to Devon, "and the first thing you do is skip class? Perhaps we need to see what your parents have to say about this." Visible Undershirt poured himself a slug of root beer and downed it.

"It's cool," said Devon. "I was in Algebra Two at my old school. Give me the other chapter tests to take home and I'll prove I'm caught up." He set his overstuffed backpack on Rourke's desk, scattering the aligned red pens.

"Problem Four," said Kelvin, clearing his throat.

Devon looked down at us. "Why, Flower Girl," he said. "Were you waiting for me?"

I smiled sweetly. "Not for *you*, you devilish thing."

"I was a little tied up earlier," he said. "Lots of new chicks to meet."

The words were obnoxious but I could feel the demon's magnetism from across the classroom. I stared over the desks into his glinting green eyes, wondering if Devon could see me. If he was in there, clawing to get out.

Desperate.

"We're doing multiplication of algebraic expressions," said Kelvin. "Your input is not required."

"Really?" said Devon. He sauntered up to Kelvin and gestured an invisible line around the seated boy. "Math with this mustardy kid?"

"How did you . . . ?" I said.

"I am completely unlike mustard," said Kelvin, "unless you mean Colonel Mustard, in which case yes, I am proud to say I am."

"Here are the two study guides, young man," said Rourke.

"You may take the chapter one test in class tomorrow and chapter two after school." He checked his cell phone. "I'd have you take chapter one right now, but I don't have time to sit here and proctor. Lucky for you. I suggest you leave my classroom now and cease being a disturbance to my tutor."

"Anytime," said Devon. He started to open his overfull backpack to put the handouts in, then stopped. He slung the backpack over one shoulder instead. It was an odd shape, big and bulgy, and the bottom of the pack looked splotched with wet. Devon tipped a hand at me, said, "Tomorrow, Flower Girl," and slouched from the room.

"Why does he call you that?" said Kelvin.

"A camellia is a flower," I said absently, still studying the retreating boy and his stuffed backpack.

"Must be one that smells nice," said Kelvin.

Mr. Rourke crumpled his root beer cup and scooped his pens into his bag. He started for the door. Past his thin button-down and out in the dim hallway I saw Devon turn the corner. Then I saw a faint light blink on and off at the top of his pack and I suddenly knew what was inside.

"Oh hells," I said. I grabbed my backpack and ran for the door, ducking past Visible Undershirt.

"Where are you—?" said Kelvin.

"I'm sorry, we'll have to work on it later, I'm sorry . . ." I called back as I dashed from the room.

"Camellia?" said Mr. Rourke. "Camellia!"

8

A Hundred Pixies

Devon vanished around the T in the hallway as I bolted from Rourke's room. Where was he going with those pixies, and why?

I was going so fast I didn't see Sparkle standing stock-still in the hallway until I turned the corner and slammed into her bony side. She stumbled backward, and something flew out of her hand and shattered into a million pieces on the floor.

"Oh hells," I said. "What'd I break? Is that a mirror? I'm sorry." I scooped up the biggest pieces, looking down the hall for Devon.

"Leave it," Sparkle said. I looked up and saw she was turned away from me, her hand covering her face.

"I bet there's a broom in the janitor's closet," I said. "Did you get cut?"

"Go away," she said. "Just go away."

I looked closer at her face, wondering if she was crying. Sparkle wasn't much of a crier even when we were kids. She got mad instead, a cold-blooded mad in which she figured out what to do to the guilty party and then did it. Like once we were getting Popsicles from the ice cream man and this third grader pushed me down and took my Bomb Pop. Next day at school, Sparkle told everyone that he had worms in his butt like a dog gets, and that no one should use the same bathroom because they would get worms, too. The teachers were cranky when the boys kept trying to use the bathroom in the other wing. But he never picked on either of us again.

The memory made me remember some of the good times we'd had, and I stayed rooted, wanting to help. Sparkle wasn't really crying, but her fingers moved just long enough to wipe one half tear, and then I saw it, though I didn't understand what I was seeing at first.

"Did you bump your nose?" I said. "It's swelling."

Sparkle's fingers left her face. She clutched the cameo necklace she always wore and glared at me. "Go ahead and laugh," she said. "Everything worked out fine for you, didn't it? Nobody cares that you don't have a dad, that you don't invite people over, that you never throw parties."

"Whoa," I said. "I don't think anyone gives two cents about your home life. It's not like *you* have anything to hide." But I still didn't understand the way her nose looked crooked to one side. "It looks like your old one," I said unthinkingly.

Sparkle raised a hand. "Get out of here now, you witch, you—"

I went from concerned to enraged. "Don't ever say that again," I said, "or you'll be sorry." And why should I apologize for breaking her mirror, anyway? She'd broken my phone yesterday and hadn't been a bit concerned.

"What are you going to do, hex me?" jeered Sparkle.

"Maybe I will," I said darkly.

Sparkle was on a roll now, venomous and stinging where she knew she could hurt me. "Did your witch mommy teach you how to work her evil spells? She's probably got you down in that basement, training to help her. With her goat's blood and her animals—"

"Stop it!" I said, trying to cover up her words, her knowledge. They bit into buried memories I refused to think about. And then I knew what I *could* do, and before she could hide her face I whipped out my phone and took a picture of Sparkle, upset and angry, wearing her old, bent nose. Her jaw fell open, the stream of words stopped. "That'll stop you from trying anything," I said. "Now I've got ammunition, too."

"Give me that," she said.

"No," I said. I held the phone out of her reach, danced backward on broken glass as she lunged for it. "Keep away," I said, jumping as her purple nails raked my bare arm. It was childish, but we were both mad and taunting each other, just like we were little again, angry over some toy.

I'm tall, but so is Sparkle. We'd both kept growing over the summer, and I don't think either of us was finished. I had maybe a half inch on her. But I used that for all it was worth and held the phone over my head, fending her off with my other arm. She backed me into the lockers and my wrist banged the wall, but I held on. "Real mature," I panted. "If I *could* work spells, you'd be the first to find out. I'd cast a spell to show the world what you're like inside."

Her teeth bared. And that's when the weirdest thing happened. We were both on our tiptoes and her fingers were touching my wrist. And then—I swear—she grew.

Not, *she jumped*, not, *she leaned forward*. She grew. And I can tell you why I know it wasn't just leaning forward. Because I swear, in that moment, her chest grew, too. It was the weirdest thing.

"Holy hells," I said. She would've totally gotten the phone away from me then, except she was equally shocked.

"What now?" she cried, and then I blinked, and she was back to normal, and I still had my phone. Sparkle stumbled back.

"Are you—?" I think I meant to say "okay." What had just happened to Sparkle? Was it something I had done? She seemed totally freaked out.

Not looking at me, Sparkle said venomously, "You show that picture to anyone and you'll regret it until you graduate."

"Then I'm keeping this until I graduate, just in case I need it," I shot back. "Call me when you grow up." I stomped down the hall, grinding bits of mirror under my heels.

I think she said, "Cash," softly, but I didn't turn around. I was keeping my strange piece of blackmail. I was tired of always knowing that she held something over me.

It wasn't just the fact that I was a stupid kid who thought the witch was my mother and that I wanted to be just like her. That stuff fades in memory.

But we'd seen the witch work a spell, and that was the sort of thing you never forgot. Not when you saw the woman you thought was your mother carry a small furry creature into the basement . . .

I stuffed down that memory, swallowed it whole. I'd refused to think about that day ever again and I wasn't going back on that now. It was time to stop Devon.

Except I had lost him.

Hells.

How was I going to find him? He could be anywhere, and the strange things that had happened around Sparkle made me horribly confused. Did the witch leave some spell on me that was going off without my knowing it? Was my close association with elementals causing rogue magic to fire, and was that even possible? The witch had said that the mannequin, with its decade of daily dragon milk, had taken on certain properties. Maybe touching the elemental in our garage day after day had left me the same. Like long exposure to radiation.

As much as I loved Moonfire, that thought made me shiver. No wonder Sparkle was freaked.

Without quite knowing where I was headed, I found myself in the drama wing. On one side of the hall was the door to the auditorium; on the other was the theater classroom. That door was half ajar and I could hear Jenah's laugh floating out. Her drama class was Sixth Hour and she often hung out afterward with the theater kids, doing those improv games I could never get the hang of.

If I went in there I could share all my problems with her. As she'd wanted me to do.

But then she'd know all my problems.

But they'd be shared.

Hells.

The classroom door moved and a flash of yellow-and-black neared it. Quicker than thought, I ducked into the auditorium and stood there, breathing. I closed my eyes and sighed. Something was deeply wrong with me. Who ducked away from her best friend like that?

As I pondered what combination of nasty ingredients made up my soul, I heard a soft thump above me. I looked up and saw the light in the costume shop was on, up in the back of the balcony.

I had been to the auditorium only a couple times to see Jenah perform, so it took me a moment to remember where the backstage stairs were to the balcony. I banged my shins into a pile of empty paint cans, which clattered all over the black stage floor. Some sleuth I was.

By the time I got up to the costume shop, it was silent. I peered left and right down the crammed length of the shop, but no one was there. I had no idea how creepy costume shops were when you were in one all by yourself. I shoved aside rows of bright polyester dresses from the sixties and satiny poof dresses from the eighties, all the while thinking a boy with a demon inside would suddenly be revealed behind a pink floral gown. Dress . . . dress . . . dress . . . demon, right?

But nothing.

I'd lost Devon, and somewhere the demon inside him was about to do something with those hundred pixies. And I was worried about what that might be.

I was about to leave when a thin draft down my rainbow T-shirt made me look up.

There was a trapdoor open to the blue October sky.

"The theater kids have roof access," I said softly. "No frikkin' way."

I climbed up the scarf-and-necklace-festooned ladder leaning against the back wall and then I was out on a tar-paper roof, staring down at the valley of the city. The city looked oddly small, a mishmash of green yards crossed with gray cement buildings and darker-gray streets, tumbling down the hill toward where I lived with a crazy witch.

But I didn't look long.

Because on the edge of the roof, arms spread wide, was Devon.

"Hells," I whispered like a prayer, and then I ran in silent, ever-quicker leaps toward the edge of the second story. Grabbed Devon's coat and toppled him sideways and backward.

Devon fell down with me, and for a moment we were entangled. He shook me off as he stood. His fingers trembled as he clutched his backpack of pixies, leaning over it like he was going to puke.

"Are you all right?" I said.

He straightened up. Raised one cool eyebrow, and for a moment I thought he was going to laugh me off again. Lie and say he was plain old Devon and then look down my shirt.

But he staggered. His shoulders lifted one at a time, as if he was steadying himself, or stepping out of something. The black faded from his hair as he bent double over his backpack again, and the word groaned from his lips: "Cam?"

"Devon? Really Devon?"

He nodded. He had a weird expression on his face, like he was trying not to barf. You know when you're concentrating so hard on not barfing that you don't have any spare attention for anything else? Yeah. That.

"How are you doing?" I put a hand on his shoulder.

"All . . . all right, I guess." He sat down hard on the roof, cradling the pixie backpack, stretching his neck from side to side, and the pukiness seemed to pass. "I think he's asleep."

I couldn't say anything more intelligent than: "Again?"

"Yeah." Devon stared across the city. "Cam, will you tell me the truth about something?"

"Yeah," I said. The October air was brisk on my bare arms, full of leaf-scented winds that whisked across the tar paper. I sat down next to him, on the alert for any sudden movements. The roof was cold through the seat of my second-favorite jeans.

"Have I been an ass all day today?" asked Devon.

"Don't you remember?" That would be creepy, if the demon was taking his memory.

Devon grimaced. "It's hard to explain. I remember most of it. Though I fell asleep a couple times when I just couldn't stay awake anymore. I tried to time that to those ancient videos in American history. I didn't want him to be the boss here at school, but really, I didn't want him to ever be the boss. I'm gonna be snorting caffeine by the time this is over, aren't I?"

"Me, too," I said.

"But the thing is, I dunno how much of what I did is stuff I would normally do. When he's awake, he must have access to my brain and memory or something. Because he knows stuff that hasn't come up. I mean, I think that's what's happening. Because this stuff comes out of my mouth that I don't think I would *want* to say, but I don't think he would *know* to say. Does that make any sense at all? And then thinking back on it, it's confusing, like I see it all as a dream."

"Weird," I said.

"He's asleep now," Devon said. "I guess he knows I want him gone, too, so he thinks he can count on me to take care of these pixies."

"Take . . . *care of*?" I said.

Devon's voice was low, tense. "He says the only way to get rid of him is to finish the contract. Is that true?" I nodded and he groaned. "Then how do I get through this contract before he eats me?" His blond hair flopped as he shook his head. "I never thought I'd be forced to choose between killing things and, uh, me. Myself."

I touched his shoulder. "I tried to stop the witch before we got to this point, but I haven't done very well so far. I didn't mess up her spell in any useful way. It's partly my fault we're here on the roof."

It would've been nice had Devon disagreed with me at this point, but he didn't. "You should've warned me," he said.

I had told him to stay in the driveway, but I let that slide. He had a lot on his mind. "I should've told you we kept an ax murderer named Clyde in the basement," I said. "That would've kept you upstairs."

He didn't laugh. He just stared into the blue-gray of the city. I guess he was savoring a moment of demon-free soul. He probably wasn't thinking about me at all. I mean, between worrying about your soul and thinking about the girl right next to you, I suppose your soul takes precedence.

"It makes me wish I could run away," he said finally. "Except he'd still be there."

"I ran away once when I was ten," I said. "Made it as far as the train station. They wouldn't sell me a ticket without an adult present. While I was scoping out the likely-looking bums, the witch materialized in the middle of the station. Literally, I mean. Her hair was all wild and frantic. I saw the look on her face and for one beautiful moment I thought it would be all, 'Oh Cam, forgive me.' But no. It was, 'Go clean the leprechaun castings out of the gutter.'"

"Cam?" Devon said.

"Yes?"

"Do you think the witch is going to kill the pixies?" he said.

I frowned, thinking of pig's ears, and a silent suppressed memory. "Probably," I said. "I mean, she said dead or alive, so that implies they'll be dead when she's done with them."

He nodded and breathed. "Okay, so part of the day when the demon took over I took a break from fighting him saying stupid things and sat and thought about this. The witch said the pixies have to be at the school on Friday. So we just have to keep them contained until Friday, and then we can let them go. I thought up here on the roof is about the safest place. So I asked your friend Jenah if there was access—"

"When did you see Jenah?"

"We have American history together," he explained. "The demon insisted on being awake all through it because some girl named Reese had a white shirt on and you could see her"—his ears went pink again, which was the surest sign I was talking to Devon—"well, her blue . . . her blue bra. And she's really, you know . . . Um. But. I got control long enough to talk to Jenah. She seems like one of those girls who knows everything that's going on."

"She is," I said.

"So if we keep the pixies up here, they'll be on-site but not dead. And your mom—"

"Not my mom."

"—didn't give a time for the pixies on Friday. And didn't say 'into my possession,' like she did with the phoenix. So Friday morning we'll simply set them free."

"Very clever," I said. "As good as a demon in wriggling around contract loopholes."

He smiled. "Do you want to see them?"

"Totally. I haven't been pixie-catching since I was a kid."

He pulled the box from his backpack and gently set it on the ground. The bowl of water had sloshed all over and the bottom of the box was wet, but he didn't seem to mind. He reached in and withdrew one tiny pixie, which he put in my palms. He didn't bother to say, "Don't let it escape," but I kept my hands cupped over the tiny thing.

"The dark green ones are from the rocky stream just before the lake," he said.

"That's a good spot." I petted the pixie's tiny curved back. It was cool and damp. He hopped a little on my palm and flicked his wings, testing them out.

"There's a footbridge there. It was just light enough to see a pair of hares. And then bats came swooping in to eat the mosquitoes, and then the pixies were swooping after the mosquitoes, too. Once the demon rubbed my eyes, I could see the pixies. See that they weren't really frogs even though they could pass for frogs. They blinked on and off like turn signals." He touched the top of my pixie's head. "We should go back there sometime."

"All right," I said, warmed by the invitation. Devon talking about animals was an entirely different person than Devon talking about bras. I wanted to say he had a similar sort of confidence to what the demon displayed, though, duh, of course he wasn't using it to try to make girls swoon, so I didn't really know how to describe what I meant. Maybe it was just tough luck for Devon that he was an animal geek—and songwriter—born into a boy-band-boy body.

Devon tugged a pencil pouch from his backpack. "I found some spiders during gym," he said, and tipped the crawly contents of the pouch into the box. "I wonder if pixies are amphibians like frogs."

"I think so," I said. "Sometime I'll show you the witch's taxonomy. It adds in the creatures regular humans don't know about."

"They don't separate them out by the creatures with magic? Maybe they should be their own kingdom." He picked out a tiny frog-pixie of his own and cupped it in his hands.

"All organisms have magic in them," I said. "Plant, animal, human. Pixies have more than frogs, but they both have magic. Like you can use frog hops for bouncing, but it takes several hundred frogs, and how often do you want to be good at bouncing? But pixie wings can be used for buoyancy or for secrecy. Or sometimes you just use their light. Their light's often used in spying spells. Capture one, get three blinks, and let it go. Witches combine ingredients through trial and error and add their own abilities to it. Scientific, really."

"You've used their wings?" said Devon.

I could hear what he thought of that in his voice. I was sure he was imagining me pulling the wings off pixies, and I almost leaped on the attack and said, "Well, you give your dog pig's ears to chew!" But then I pulled myself back from that paranoid response and said calmly, "Pixies die with the first snowfall. Their wings slough off. You gather them in the snow."

"Could the demon use these little guys for spells, too?"

"I dunno if he'd bother," I said. "Elementals don't work magic, they *are* magic. Unlike witches, they don't need ingredients to perform magic, because it comes from within. But I don't know what the rules are right now, while he's inside you. Witchipedia was vague on that part. And by 'vague,' I mean the article had been edited a whole lot, back and forth. I guess demons don't like to have too much written up about them."

Devon nodded. "He said he didn't have any power, but I don't think that's true," he said. "He already showed me pixies that I couldn't see before. Who knows what else he can do." His pixie blinked on and off in his palms as he gazed out over the city.

"Friday," I said firmly. "You just have to make it to Friday."

He nodded. "Just resist him, over and over. Not let him find my weak spots."

"You think you can?"

"Sure," he said. But his eyes told a different story, I thought. "He's not going to get the best of me. He'd have to know—" He looked around like someone might be coming up behind him. "Stupid of me. I know where he is and he can hear everything. He knows anything we plan. He'll be able to recall anything I say to you."

"Anything?" I said. My heart went *patter-thud.*

That needed no answer, I guess. Devon didn't say anything. We sat on the edge of the rooftop together and watched the red and yellow trees sway against the blue sky. I could see small figures walking around in the park across the street. The box of pixies blinked.

"He thinks he can seduce me by making a hundred girls fall for me. I don't care about that. Who'd want to be clung to by ordinary everyday girls?"

"Not I."

"But then sometimes," Devon said softly to the trees in front of us, "he's got the confidence to say the things I maybe wanted to say, but didn't have the guts. It gets very confusing."

"Um, really?" I said. His hand was very close to mine on the rooftop. Our arms were so close that when we breathed out at the same time, my sleeve touched his jacket. There seemed to be electricity jumping that gap, from his arm to mine, heating my side. I wondered if he could see me breathing. The more I thought about the way our breathing made our sleeves touch, the more I seemed to mess up my own breathing patterns, making my breaths seem irregular and hugely obvious. Surely he could see the uncool way my chest lurched, just from our stupid sleeves.

Why couldn't I just enjoy sitting on the school roof with a rather nice boy who had a few demonic issues? Why did I have to be thinking about my stupid breathing?

I blamed the witch.

"Hells!" I said as my pixie made a dash for it. I lunged and caught the little guy, placed my finger gently between his wings and held. He blinked faster, upset with me.

Devon yawned. "I haven't been this beat-up since I tried to walk six dogs at once."

"How'd that work out?"

"Got my arms and legs wrapped around a birch tree," Devon said. "Sat there with six dogs licking my face while Dad untangled me. I got a song out of it, though." He sighed. "We'd better get off the roof while the gettin's good. Pack these pixies up."

My mouth wanted to say something dumb like, "I hope you're not bored with me," but I kept my lips tightly sealed. "Did you have somewhere you needed to be?" I said lamely.

"Need to schedule practice with the band before Friday," he said. "Demon or no, I don't want us to suck."

"I'm sure you won't suck."

"Not if I let him sing for me. Maybe I'll get one good thing out of him." Devon's arm moved as he put his pixie in the box. The electricity left my space. "Cam?" he said. "About Friday . . ."

How dumb is it that I hoped he'd ask me to the dance? Very dumb. We had more important things on our minds. Anyway, I still liked him better with the black hair than with the blond, which meant I was all kinds of weird, liking something that was demon related. I had problems I wasn't going to admit to Devon.

"You'll be there, right?" Devon said. "Help me if things go haywire?"

Internally I sighed. "Of course," I said. He reached for my pixie and I put the little winged creature into his hands. Our fingers touched as he took it from me. Electricity, *bam.*

I kept waiting for him to pull his hands away, but he didn't. It was like we were both pretending that a pixie needed four hands to keep it from getting away. His face was so near to mine, his green eyes clear and deep. "Then . . . maybe after . . ."

I tumbled over sideways as the backpack I was leaning on was jerked out from under me. "What the—"

Sparkle backed away, rifling through the swiped backpack.

"Get back here," shouted Devon, and I heard him jumping to recapture the newly escaped pixie.

I started toward Sparkle, but she glared at me and I stopped, thrown.

Her nose was back to normal.

I mean current-normal. The nice straight nose she'd had the last two months.

"Erase the picture and I'll go," Sparkle said.

"It's not in there." I edged toward her. Sparkle hefted the backpack as if she would throw it. Her eyes were wide, darting. I knew it would be bad for me to show Sparkle any empathy, but I couldn't help it. "Are you okay?" I said. "You seem really weird the last couple days. Weirder than normal." The barb soothed the meaner urges of my soul.

"You'd know weird," she sniped. "Where's your phone?"

In my pocket, thank goodness, but I didn't want another wrestling match. "In my locker," I said. "Can I have my back-pack?"

"Cam," said Devon.

"Picture first," Sparkle shouted. "I want it gone, gone, all evidence of weird stuff gone, do you hear? Gone for good! I want it to never have existed. Erase it!"

"Calm, calm," I said. "What's really going on here, Sparkle?"

"Cam," repeated Devon, lower and deeper.

One hand flew to her cameo, the other pointed past me. "Tell me what's really going on with *him*."

I whirled and there was a different Devon standing there. He fell into a crouch, his eyes were hard. Black hair flopped, fingers curled into claws around the recaptured pixie.

The demon had woken up.

9

Squash

"Thanks for filling the first task," the demon said. He stretched. "It's a rather odd and tingly feeling, being bound to a contract. I've done it before, of course, but it's new and different every time. Isn't it?" He leered at Sparkle.

"We wouldn't know," I said. "Your 'frogs' are up here, so why don't you come down off the roof and go home for the night? Sparkle, I suggest you move along, too." I motioned us all across the roof to the trapdoor, but nobody budged.

"Task one is not entirely complete," Estahoth said.

"Aha," I said. "Devon figured out that the 'frogs' just have to be here till Friday, then we can let them go. You should be in favor of that, because as I understand it, your kind likes to avoid completing contracts. Now off we go, down from the roof." I had to get the demon away from those pixies.

"Quite right," said Estahoth. "But the reason we like to avoid completing contracts is so we can stay longer. Your mother has worked in a time limit of Halloween. No extensions. Thus all my energies are focused on *him*." He thumped his chest and a scent of firecracker and mold wafted out.

"Camellia?" said Sparkle. "What on earth is the new boy going on about?" She clutched her cameo necklace like a security blanket.

"Please. Go," I said. I crossed to the trapdoor and motioned her down it. She stepped onto the rung of the ladder, but didn't go any farther. My nerves were on edge and the little hairs on my arms stood upright. "Devon, you come, too." I tried the witch's firm tone.

The demon pointed a finger at Sparkle. "I know something you don't know," he said in a singsongy taunt, and as his finger stayed on her, her face seemed to change, but not just her nose this time, not just her height. Her face aged rapidly, wrinkles forming, jowls drooping. He waggled his finger and then she went back the other way, younger, younger, shrinking. Back up.

"I'm . . . going to . . ." Sparkle said, all green and white, and then she slid/fainted down the ladder into the costume room.

"Hells," I said. "Sparkle?" I stepped onto the rungs of the ladder to see if she was broken or bleeding.

But the instant I did that, the demon laughed and swooped down on the cardboard box.

"You give that here," I said firmly. "We told you the contract was safe."

"Just as the old phoenix has to die so the new one can be born," said the demon. "Just so, we will remake Devon in a new image." He uncurled his hand and revealed my dark green froggy pixie, dangling by its leg. It blinked rapidly, its wings fluttered. "*Crush* the old."

I grabbed for handholds to climb back up, but the demon was suddenly there, and he kicked my shoulder hard. I slammed down onto the ladder, my armpit hitting the roof.

The demon loomed above, his hair rippling wildly. "No," said Devon, forcing the words out of unmoving lips. His eyes were ringed in stricken white. "No!" His hand closed around the frightened pixie. Closed tighter, tighter. A small leg waved frantically.

"No!" I shouted, and grabbed Devon's pant leg, tried to haul myself out, tried to stop the inevitable. But the demon kicked me free, and then a horrid pressure feeling settled on my head, as if I were being pushed down by hurricane winds. The pressure shoved me, shouting, down the hole and slammed the trapdoor on my head. My fingers slipped on the scarves and beads draped over the ladder. My feet skidded to the floor—I thought I would land on Sparkle, but there was no one there. A wire clothes hanger gouged my arm as I tumbled backward onto my hip.

I heard a muffled squeak—and then the pixie was silent. Everything was silent. Then came a strange sound of hysteria— like someone caught between tears and savage laughter, switching between the two.

I stormed up the ladder and pushed and shoved on the trapdoor. Pried with a coat hanger around the edges. Banged on it with a cowboy boot.

The trapdoor would not budge.

I had to wait twenty minutes for the next bus, and then it was another fifteen to get home. Devon didn't show up at the bus stop. I sat by myself on a mottled brown seat and brooded, near tears and rage all at once. Whenever I calmed, the memory of Devon's stricken face as the demon made him kill the pixie would set me off again. I was so furious at the witch I wanted to scream, long and loud without stopping.

I didn't. I made it off the bus without breaking down in public. I even said thanks to the bus driver.

But the rage and tears coursing through me explained, though not excused, why I was horribly rude to the small form in yellow and black waiting on the doorstep.

"What do you want?" I said.

"Sunshine and butterflies," said Jenah. She snapped the knees of her fishnets, adjusting them as she got up. "Pretty rose-colored auras shot with streaks of gold. But mostly, to talk."

"Thanks," I said, spitting the words out. "I have nothing to talk about." I just wanted her to go. Everything the witch touched turned to disaster, and it was now spreading rapidly. Anyone that tried to help me would get brought down by my home life. Jenah needed to give up on me and *go*.

"Your hair looks like flying pigs hit it," said Jenah.

I ignored this and put my key in the lock.

"Did you hide from me in the auditorium earlier?" said Jenah.

"What? No."

"I thought I saw the back of your shirt." She touched it. "I called after you."

"Not everything's about you," I said, the desperate words tearing out. Couldn't she see that she was going to bring trouble on herself? My secrets needed to stay secret. Jenah eyed me and I calmed my voice. "I have to go," I said, trying to squish down the storm of feelings. "Really. I'll see you tomorrow."

I ducked in and shut the door on Jenah. I didn't expect to be in trouble with the witch for being late, because I'd texted her about staying late for algebra tutoring. No, the latest problem was Moonfire. The witch's horrible tasks for the demon meant I was late for my chores with the dragon for the second day in a row, and Moonfire couldn't take care of all her needs stuck in that garage. I let Wulfie out the front door to find his favorite bush, and hurried out the back.

Where I ran smack into the witch. Fury flamed. "You horrible, horrible—" I started.

"Your algebra teacher called," said the witch. She rose from the stone bench near the pumpkin vines and dusted off her peach pencil skirt.

"Hells," I said, derailed.

"He wants me to come in and talk about your grades," Sarmine said. "He says you're too good a student to let algebra slide."

"I am not letting it slide," I said, aggravated. "I did badly on my test but I went in to study with Kelvin. But I had to leave studying with Kelvin because of *your* demon problem, and that's when Rourke got cranky enough to call you. He'll never let me make up the test now."

"Why didn't you just leave a doppelgänger to sit with this Kelvin person while you did the important things? I know you know the doppelgänger spell. You helped gather the ingredients when I used it to avoid that dreadful neighborhood block party. Five werewolf hairs, easily collected from Wulfie. One pint of cream. One huff of dog's breath. Two—"

Her list infuriated me. The witch could get under my skin faster than anybody in the world. "For your information, you have to be a witch to perform that spell. And are you seriously saying that my solution to algebra is to skip out on the tutor? What kind of crazy person are you? You don't care two cents what happens to my grades, as long as I gather your ingredients and keep track of your demons."

"I merely pointed out the way to keep this Rourke character from being angry at you," said the witch. The October wind whisked around us. "As I judge your developing character, you are determined to keep your grades up whether or not you have my support. Thus I save my energy for making you realize that there are other things in life besides human schooling." She frowned. "As for your chores, I don't understand your position. I give you all the best tasks and take the mundane ones of cooking and dishwashing myself. Do you know that my mother used to have me scrub out the bathtubs? Like a regular human? With a *sponge*?"

Sarmine on a rant about her mother could go on for ages. I interrupted this digression. "So you think other things in life are more important," I said. "Like what, settling scores against old enemies? How does causing chaos at school—*my* school— give you the moral high ground? Just so you know, your tasks are wreaking havoc on Devon. I have half a mind to thwart the demon by stopping him from completing his tasks."

"You have half a mind, period," said the witch. "A transfigured phoenix is still a phoenix."

The wind sent a chill down my spine. "You mean it's still going to burst into fire?"

"It will explode on Halloween," said the witch, "whether we've found where Kari hid it or not. Uncontained phoenix fire will disintegrate your entire school and anyone unlucky enough to be inside the building at the time. I suggest you and your delicate little morals consider that." She pulled a small packet of dried pepper from her fanny pack and sprinkled it over one of my pumpkins. The wind tickled my nose, along with the pepper dust. I knew I was supposed to ask the witch what spell she was creating, so she could impart some sort of "valuable" lesson about the properties of dried pepper or whatever.

"I have a dragon to tend to," I said coldly. I pushed past the witch and stalked toward the garage.

"At least I'm doing something with my life," said the witch from behind me. "You should've seen me at your age. Able to work complicated spells, already creating new ones. Causing chaos from here to the Pacific Ocean."

"I'm so happy for you."

"And my sister Belarize was even faster. When she was eight and I was four she decided she was sick of being ousted as the youngest. She planted a monster under my bed that almost took my foot clean off. Mother refused to believe my sister had done it. She had a blind spot about Belarize's lack of morals. You *don't turn on your family.*" Sarmine harrumphed at the memory, then rounded on me, throwing up her hands. "I just don't know how to get past your blind spot, Camellia! I give you spells, you reject them. I show you counterspells, you don't even try. Your attitude toward witchery keeps me up at night. Don't you know what happens to weak witches? Don't you understand how cruel the witch world is?"

"I'm not a witch!" I turned and shouted. "Why does everyone keep saying I am? I'm not like you. I'm not like the horrible way you behave. Nothing at all. I'm *not*!"

"You stubborn, blind—" Sarmine breathed out. Her face calmed. All cold and stoic it got, and her hands were steel on her wand. "There's going to be a punishment for this . . . for this algebra mess." It seemed like she'd wanted to say something else, but no. Only mean-just-because Sarmine would say in the same breath that algebra was useless and then punish me for it. "Not for failing your test, but for putting me in the annoying position of having to talk to this Rourke character."

"No!" I shouted, stomping through the grass, bearing down on her. "I'm sick of your punishments. You have no right—"

"Half an hour mummified by the pumpkin plants ought to do it," she said.

She plucked one hair from my head, and while I said, "Ouch, what the hell?" she doused it with a spray bottle from her fanny pack, dropped it on the peppered and god-knows-what-else pumpkin, and tapped it with her dragon-milk wand.

Instantly the vines spiraled up, reaching for me. One vine lassoed my arm.

"Oh *hells*," I said. I yanked my arm out of the tightening pumpkin noose and ran, but a vine coiled around my ankle. I thunked to my knees. Another vine plonked over my shoulders, and its leaves thumped on top of my head. "Let me out!" I shrieked.

"If you'd studied your self-defense spell, you could stop me now," Sarmine said.

I clawed and tore, but more vines coiled around my limbs, rolling me into the middle of the pumpkin patch. My shoulder hurt where the demon had kicked me. A small green pumpkin bonked my nose. "Get back here!"

I think she said something like "It's clime you faced up to da tooth," but I couldn't hear very well with the giant pumpkin leaves stuffing my ears.

My flailing hand struck an overripe pumpkin and smashed into pumpkin guts. "Sarmine!" I shouted, and then a huge wad of leaves stuffed my mouth, and I choked and stopped yelling. At least I had an airhole for my nose, or I'd really be in trouble.

The vines rolled me over one more time and my nose smashed into dirt. I arched, stretching my neck out of the dirt to breathe, snorting out compost and probably bug bits. I tried not to panic as mulch clung to my nose with my inhaled breaths. Why did my life suck so hard? Flunking algebra, falling for a demon-boy, and finally, smothered to death by a rabid pumpkin.

I wasn't going to save the world from the witch. I couldn't even save myself. And who would slop out poor Moonfire's garage now? Catch the witch doing it. Oh, she liked having the dragon milk and scales around, but what about the dragon herself?

I loved my dragon. I was the one who took care of her. We were going to fly away some day and find both of our families, by hook or by crook—

At this point I realized I was getting light-headed. But the image of me flying dragonback grew stronger and more appealing. Flying through the air, just flying, flying, flying. Air. Blue sky. Abyss. So . . . pretty—

Hands grabbed my ankles, dislodging my nose from the dirt. I sucked in great snorts of air, and then coughing, muffle-shrieked through the leaves. I kicked, and then whoever was grabbing my ankles sat on my shins. A shearing sound, and then my arm was free, and then I realized that someone was letting me out, so I stopped trying to kick whoever it was and concentrated on that lovely stuff called air going in my nose. I tensed my fist, just in case.

The leaves stuffed into my mouth pulled apart and I spit bits of chlorophyll and gasped whole mouthfuls of lovely, lovely air. "Who—?" Choke, sputter. "What—?"

"Sssh," said a familiar voice, and then the leaves blinding me were cut away and I saw it was Jenah, holding a pair of hair-cutting scissors, now dripping with green.

"Jenah. Thank goodne—I mean, I told you never to come here," I said. "Why didn't you listen to me and go home?"

"Ohmigod, *seriously*?" Jenah said. Her chic black haircut was straggly around her face, clumpy with pumpkin leaf juice. I had never seen it untidy. "I was walking down the street, unloved and unwanted, when I felt a sudden shift in the world, like a magnetic force drawing me back. I looked through the fence and saw the mother of all great pumpkins rolling you up like a veggie wrap. And *then* I had to duck behind your stupid thornbushes until your aunt drove off before I could climb over the fence and cut you out of the squash. My favorite shirt is stained with pumpkin pulp, my fishnets are torn and!—I think your fence tried to eat me. At the absolute-most-subpar least you are now going to say: 'Thank you, Jenah.'"

"Thanks," I said. "I'm very grateful. Now will you get out of here before Sarmine comes back and catches you?" I brushed prickly bits of vines and leaves from my jeans.

Jenah folded her arms and eyed me. "No," she said.

"Funny. Get."

"I've been chill long enough," said Jenah. "Whatever's going on here is different—I mean *different*—and it doesn't have anything to do with the color of your aunt's bedspread. You are straining our friendship, Camellia."

The walls of my privacy were tumbling down around me. "Can't I have my space? What does it hurt you?" I backed away from the patch.

"Friends help each other when they have big troubles. If you can't trust me—"

"If you weren't so *nosy*! Who watches their friends through the fence?" I was being so unfair but I couldn't stand the thought of explaining my life, sharing the secrets I'd protected for so long.

"—then you don't think I'm really your friend," Jenah finished. She brushed back sticky strands of hair, and her eyes were reproachful. "Nosy? *Really*? I mean, obviously I am. But am I really off base here? Something's wrong and I want to help you."

And you're nosy, I thought, but I didn't say it. Jenah did want to know everything about everyone. But . . . she also meant it when she said she wanted to help. I knew that.

I just didn't know if she'd still mean it once she knew the truth.

But it didn't matter. Sometimes you reach the breaking point, where you have to spill everything that you're holding back. Out of all the people in the world, Jenah was the one I could most trust.

"Please," she said.

I squinched my eyes shut and forced it out: "My aunt is a witch and Devon is possessed by a demon."

"Is that poetic description?"

"Aunt Sarmine summoned a demon to help her take over the city. It was supposed to go into a mannequin, but when Devon interrupted the spell, it went into him, and now if I don't come up with something clever it's going to eat all of Devon's soul and be inside him forever."

I could tell that Jenah wanted to believe all this. It wasn't

the same as all that aura stuff, but it wasn't like she was totally unprepared for the idea of mystic unknowns, either. Not
to mention that she'd just seen a pumpkin try to eat me. She
wanted to believe.

I cut to the chase.

I took that vial of unicorn sanitizer out of my backpack and
flicked three drops on Jenah.

The air sparkled around my best friend. The pumpkin juice
disappeared from her yellow-and-black shirt, the sticky sap fell
from her hair. In a moment she was clean and pressed and spar-
kling around the edges, as if she were an anime princess.

"I can't do anything about your torn fishnets," I said. "Sorry."

"Oh. My. God," said Jenah. She boggled at her shirt. "This
is going to take lots of re-sorting along the astral planes."

"Yeah, well," I said. I fiddled with my shirt hem. "You see
why I don't want to talk about it."

Jenah touched her shiny clean hair, marveling. "So next you're
gonna stop the demon with witch magic?"

I shuddered. "In the first place, I am not a witch, so don't
even think it. Anyone can use unicorn sanitizer because that
stuff is powerful. Sarmine and I are not even related."

"I thought she was your aunt."

"I call her my aunt because the long story is too complicated to go into. It's easier to say I live with my aunt than to
say I live with a witch who stole me from my real parents.
Anything that causes fewer questions, that's what I go with,
okay? When I was really little and didn't know any better I
thought she was my mom." I turned on the hose and washed
my hands and face. No point in wasting valuable sanitizer
on me.

"Mmm," said Jenah.

"And secondly, not even Sarmine can work magic on the demon." I gargled and spat out pumpkin-leaf water. My mouth

still felt prickly. "A demon isn't human or animal. It's an elemental. Only elementals can affect other elementals."

"What the heck is an elemental?"

"Well, a witch *does* magic, but an elemental is *made of* magic. There's three types of elementals, and there's a witch saying about them. 'Dragon, phoenix, and demon fell; these three a witch cannot bespell.'" I toweled myself dry with my hoodie. "Normally demons don't live among us, or we'd have bigger problems. They're the earth elementals and they live, like, in the molecules of the core of the Earth, where they swim around in the fire and annoy each other. They're trapped there, unless a witch opens up a passage for them. Dragons are right here on earth, and phoenix are air creatures, though apparently one is transfigured and imprisoned somewhere in the school . . ." I stopped, because Jenah was looking at me funny. "Which part was too much for you?"

"Dragons," she said, and she looked all swoony. "Are dragons really real?"

"Yes. Though they're endangered. I dunno how many are left."

"Have you ever seen one?"

I grinned. A strange and marvelous feeling swept through me. "Would you say I owed you something for saving my life from the Great Rabid Pumpkin?" I said.

1Ø

Jenah Hearts Dragons

Relief at sharing my life with *someone* made me feel all giddy, like I'd just gone whooshing down the slide at the water park, or like that feeling when you suddenly *know* your crush likes you, and you light up from head to toe.

Joy. Ridiculous joy. Relief.

That's how I felt now as I watched Jenah's face light up at the sight of Moonfire. "Do you really see her?" I said.

"Of course. Why not?"

Which made me wonder if maybe Jenah really did see auras, or if there was more magic in regular humans than the witch claimed. Either way, remove one more thing that had made me feel different. Jenah could see the dragon, and Jenah knew about my life.

I mean, it's not like her knowing was going to measurably help the situation of living with the witch or of stopping the demon in Devon.

But that didn't matter. I still felt like my whole messed-up life had more hope than it did half an hour ago.

After I checked to make sure Wulfie had made it back inside, I told Jenah the whole story from the beginning while I slopped out the garage and she petted the dragon's warm hide. Moonfire purred, and before long Jenah got comfortable enough to drape herself along the dragon's translucent side, in full-body contact with the thrums.

When I got to the part about crashing into Sparkle in the

hallway, I pulled out my phone and showed Jenah the picture of ol' Right-Angle Nose.

"Spooky," said Jenah. "I don't understand it."

"Me neither," I said. "But I'm hanging on to it. Anything that helps me balance out what she knows about me . . . What?"

"Not to put mustard in your aura," said Jenah, "but you could've photoshopped it."

"I didn't. Sparkle knows it, too."

"If she thinks about it, she'll realize that's an easy way out for her."

I surveyed my phone glumly. "Photographic proof ain't what it used to be."

"Not when images can be anything you want," said Jenah. "Change reality with a mouse click. Pretty much like magic, isn't it?"

"It is not," I said. "Magic is evil." The memory of the fight with the witch overwhelmed me with rage. "And Sarmine keeps wanting me to work evil spells like her, which is doubly stupid, because she knows perfectly well I don't have witch blood."

Jenah cradled her fishnetted knees. "Have you tried any spells?"

"No." I glared at her. "And don't start with that maybe-we're-really-related thing. I told you we aren't. You don't know what I saw when I was five."

"You found out you were stolen?" said Jenah.

"Let's just say that Sparkle and I saw her perform one of her particularly nasty spells," I said. "That's when I knew we weren't alike. At all."

Jenah pondered this. "Okay," she said. "But that wasn't what I was going to say. You mentioned several times that witches are paranoid and hide things from each other and the world, and honestly, probably from themselves, too. Right?"

"So?"

"So maybe the thing about having to have witch blood isn't strictly true," Jenah said. Moonfire arched her neck and Jenah resumed her scale skritching. "Maybe that's one of those paranoid lies witches spread to keep their secrets safe."

"I'm not sure," I said. "Though it doesn't seem totally off base, either." I picked up the bristle brush and began scrubbing sheep bits off the garage wall. (You try tearing into a whole sheep with dragon jaws.)

"You were surprised I could see Moonfire," Jenah pointed out. Suddenly she sat up straight. "Holy cow," she said. "Is the dragon talking to me?"

"Did you see something?"

"A dragon flying over a mountain range. Settling in a cliff high up. Looking out to sea. Is that her?"

I put down the scrub brush and looked at Jenah with renewed admiration. "I don't think everybody can understand her," I said. "I mean, I can, but I've grown up with her."

"And I know *I* don't have witch blood," said Jenah. "It's like when I sense auras. Except a trillion times clearer and more obvious." She settled back against the dragon again, closing her eyes. "I think she's glad to meet me. I get a sense of . . . lonely?"

You've probably realized I'm not perfect by now. (I know, right?) One of the traits I hate more than anything is jealousy. But every so often it tries to sneak in. I stomped on the twinge that tickled my belly, hard. I was glad Jenah could commune with Moonfire. I was glad it came naturally for her, and apparently clearer and better than for me. At least, I was determined to be glad. I attacked the sheep stain with firm scrubs.

"She *is* lonely," I said. "She misses her kind. The last few female dragons."

"It's probably hard being imprisoned here," Jenah said, not pointedly, just thinking out loud.

"She's not . . ." But then I stopped. I mean, I'd always thought of her as sort of a pet. But she couldn't be, not really. Elementals had human intelligence, and humans couldn't be pets.

Wulfie was an abandoned cub that the witch rescued. One of her few good deeds, though we'll have a heckuva time figuring out how to send him to kindergarten, with him being human only once a month. I was unfairly and maliciously bartered for. Wulfie and I would have a hard time leaving till we were eighteen and legal in the human system, but other than that we weren't slaves and we weren't pets.

But what about the dragon? Was she free to go?

I leaned against the wall, flipping the brush back and forth between my hands. The wall was cold on my back, but the dragon's heat was warm from the front. Like a campfire. "Ask her . . . ." I said slowly. "Ask her if she likes it here."

Jenah was silent, listening. "She says the garage is as good as a cave," she said, "And also she has one friend here. That's you."

Warmth flooded me. "Tell her I love her, too."

"She likes being with you, especially when you understand her pictures. But . . ."

"What?"

"She misses her friends. She's sad not to know if they're all dead or not. She thinks about them every day." Jenah paused. "Every time she shows 'them' it seems to have 'female' associated with it?"

"Male dragons were apparently very nasty," I said. "And more visible. We're pretty sure they're all dead. Elementals don't die of old age, but they can be hunted and killed."

"She doesn't have a way to call them. Her—something like radar?—won't go far enough. There could be more sister dragons farther away that she doesn't know about. She can't—boost her signal, I guess it is—any higher."

"Let me listen," I said. I settled in next to Jenah, and got images I was familiar with, of a dragon's-eye view in the sky, of Moonfire soaring and looking for someone like her. But as usual, the images were faded and flickering for me, whereas Jenah seemed to feel aloft. Her eyes were closed in wonder as the dragon dipped and flew.

"One by one, she lost contact with her friends," Jenah narrated, in longer sentences now as she grew more comfortable with the dragon's mode of communication. "More people settled here. Most of them couldn't see her, but sometimes people could. Witches, of course. And other people, too. They hunted her. This went on for a long time. Then one night, exhausted from a flight from a man who was hunting her, she flew straight into a storm. Her wing tangled on a power line and broke. She sent out a distress signal, and that's when she met Sarmine. Sarmine offered her a safe place to stay in exchange for her milk and discarded scales."

I saw that image crystal clear, with a young Sarmine, almost as young as me, in a T-shirt and a ponytail. Another house, one I didn't recognize. A man raking the yard while a smiling Sarmine painted that other garage a familiar shade of sky blue.

"Sometimes she wants to leave, but she gets worried about being chased by men with guns again. So she stays. Because what's out there anyway to look forward to?"

"Poor Moonfire," I said. I toyed with the brush bristles. "Stuck here in a witch's garage, nothing to look forward to but two more centuries of giving the witch her milk, till the witch kicks the bucket. I haven't even gotten the demon to come look at her lungs."

"The not knowing, that's the worst," murmured Jenah.

Tears splashed into the glass jars hung around the dragon's face.

"See, that would be cool," I said. "If I *were* a witch, I could do awesome spells like trying to help the dragon find her friends. Working toward good in the world. Like Alphonse, but without the breaking and entering. That's what I'd do."

"I don't see why you couldn't," said Jenah. "If you were a witch, of course. Or if spells worked for anybody. Then you could do them."

If I could do spells. The thought sent strange shivers up my spine, and for the first time since I was five they weren't shivers of horror. What if I could do *good* things with spells? Use them to help people, to help animals? What if I could do things that were the opposite of Sarmine?

But no, that's not what real witches did. I'd seen that often enough. Being a witch corrupted you just like having a demon inside you did. Power ate away at your soul. "Did you see Sarmine's trick with the pumpkin patch?" I said. "That's what real witches are like. Conceited paranoid monsters, who'd as soon punish you as look at you." Devon was just dying with that horrid thing in him and there was nothing I could do about it as a plain ordinary human. Help him with the tasks, stop him from the tasks, it didn't seem to matter. I couldn't do a darn thing to stop Devon's soul from getting eaten. I smacked the floor with the brush. "This sucks."

Jenah stroked the dragon's hide and considered. "You said that when the spell went wrong, the witch tried to shove Devon in the pentagram to trap him. Is there some way you could trick the demon into a pentagram?"

I scrambled up. "Hey! That's not a bad idea. I trick him into a pentagram and that contains both of them. But then what?" I paced the length of the garage, kicking the straw. The demon was going to be around till the phoenix explosion on Halloween, regardless. If I captured Devon and the demon in a pentagram, that would stop the demon from doing bad things. Which might help Devon . . . or, it might not. Being stuck in a pentagram would stop the demon from things like squishing pixies, but it wouldn't stop the demon from whispering things into Devon's mind, poisoning his soul.

"It's not just a little spell I need," I said slowly. I remembered my Witchipedia research, and the idea I had dismissed before. "I need a really powerful spell. I need a spell to get the demon out of Devon. If a spell got him in, there must be a spell to get him out. If I can find it." That would be something good I could do, something *right*. "That doesn't solve the exploding phoenix, though."

"Well, you have till Friday for that," said Jenah.

"It's Wednesday."

"Trying to be helpful," said Jenah. "How easy are spells? A matter of tapping something with a wand?"

"God, no. Even if you're right that I can do it, I still have to track down a spell and then puzzle it out." I thought of the rooftop again. Of banging a boot against the trapdoor while the demon made Devon kill that little pixie so horribly. How many had had the demon made him squish? I plonked the bristle brush into my palm. "I'm going to try. The witch wants me to work a spell? Fine. I'll figure out how to save Devon. That's the kind of spell I want to do."

I swallowed hard at the thought of trying spells, but it had to be done. "Time to step up the game."

After Jenah reluctantly left, I checked to make sure the witch was still gone. I didn't know where she'd gone, but she despised normal people too much to ever stay out for very long. I checked on Wulfie—he was curled up with his tail over his nose on the living room couch.

And then I snuck into the witch's study, accessible only from her bedroom. Honestly, I was surprised that she didn't have any spells to stop me from going in there.

Well.

No spells that I *saw*, anyway.

The witch had already been gone longer than I expected, and I didn't want to push my luck further, so I hurried. I tugged book after book from the shelf and thumbed through them, scanning for something obvious. A lot of the books seemed not to be spells at all, but boring political treatises about ecology and the Witch Government. I shoved those back, and also ignored the stacks of trashy witch romances. There was a media tie-in with Zolak the demon hunter in a ripped-up shirt on the cover. After I finished being squicked that the witch had the same crush I did, Zolak's black hair and knowing look reminded me of demon-infused Devon. I wished yet again that my phone would phone real-world phones or connect to the real-world Internet. Devon must be at home and miserable while the demon planned his next round of attacks. I wished I could tell him I was thinking of him. Reluctantly I shelved the book, though I thought when all this was over, I might sneak it out sometime.

In contrast to the romances, the spellbooks were covered in layers of dust and cobwebs. I was kind of surprised, because the witch is such a neat freak about important things. I wondered if she was getting lazy, ignoring this library of information—or if she already knew everything in these books. Or, if she'd already judged which books were useful and which were heaps of lies, like the Web sites of silly egotistical witches all over WitchNet.

I shut down that worry. I had enough unknowns with this trying-to-do-a-spell thing without wondering whether or not the witch's books were accurate. Maybe I didn't know as much as Sarmine did, but I knew Sarmine, and she would *not* have books around that were heaps of lies.

I took one book that had general information on phoenix, and another about dragon history. An antique one called *The Young Witch's Handbook to Building a WitchRadio* (useless for the demon problem, but I thought it might have something about dragon communication in it). I stacked them both on top of a couple of encyclopedic-looking books.

And then I saw the book I needed.

From the looks of it, it was a very well (and recently) read book on demons, but when my fingers came near, it jumped to another shelf. I grabbed again—and it jumped again.

That might be enough to stop an ordinary book browser, but it wasn't going to stop me. I read the spine of the book next to it out loud: "*Witch's Passion: A Fiery Tale.* That sounds promising." I focused my thoughts and my left hand on *Witch's Passion*. The demon book twitched a little as I neared it. I grabbed *Witch's Passion*'s spine . . . and then with my right hand I pounced on the demon book. "Aha!"

It struggled, but as soon as it was off the bookshelf it went limp. "You're mine now," I told it.

I nudged the other books on the shelf closer to each other, wiped away fingerprints in the dust . . . and then I saw a small black wand behind a glass door in the bookcase.

Of course.

If I wanted to work a spell, I needed a wand.

But was the witch going to miss this one? It was behind glass. It must be important. I glanced around the study to see if she had any others. I only ever saw her use her slim aluminum one. I had no idea she had other wands at all.

That's when I heard the garage door click.

I swear, it was like she had radar, like the dragon.

I grabbed the wand from the shelf and closed the glass door. Then hightailed it back to my room and shoved it and the books under my bed, just as her heels clicked down the hallway. They went past my room to hers and I breathed a tentative sigh of relief.

I was dying to look at the books, but I still had the second half of *The Crucible* to read, a chapter of biology, and two work sheets for French I. Not to mention that stupid algebra. Boldly, I decided to do algebra first, and started off on problem four of the study guide for the test I hoped Rourke would let me re-take. Now what had Kelvin said? He'd said I could do it if I went slow, right?

Laboriously, I wrote down all the things I knew. Crossed out all the things I didn't need. Then arranged the problem into the equations I needed, using my finger as a placeholder.

By problem six I was starting to think that Kelvin was right.

I'd thought of algebra as something requiring great intuitive leaps and an inner aptitude, because that's the way Rourke had been doing it. But all this was step by step. Anyone who figured out how to slot all the witch's bizarro demands into one stream-lined schedule and then check them off could do something that was step by step.

Thank you, Kelvin, I thought. I was going to have to tell him tomorrow that I appreciated him.

I started on problem seven, and then there was a sort of ring-ing noise in my backpack. Everyone else in the entire world would have known what it was immediately, but do you know why it took me forever to figure out what it was? Because I'd never had a single solitary phone call on my cell phone before. Because—as you probably remember—my phone was hooked in *only* to the witch system. Sarmine hated talking on the phone, so she only texted me those awful BRING ME A BIRD sorts of messages, and like, what, was I going to give the number to the creepy witch guy who raised unicorns and once drooled on my shoe? I thought not.

Big surprise number two: It was Devon.

"How on earth are you able to call this phone?" I said.

"The demon arranged it," Devon said. "He had some charming doublespeak for his new strategy with me but basically it's carrot and stick. He does something awful, then he gives me something I want. Back and forth. He said he'd go to sleep now but he hasn't yet. Maybe we'll have to bore him into it."

I laughed, warmed at the idea that calling me was something Devon wanted. Then sobered. "How are you doing since the rooftop?"

Pause. "All right," he said.

He clearly didn't want to talk about the pixies, so I changed the subject, even though I didn't know if it was better for him to ignore it or not. "Did you have a lot of homework?"

"No," he said. "Estahoth did it. It was one of his carrots."

"Are you sure it's right?" I said.

"Yes, because the interesting thing is, I remember doing it. I have all that information in my head. It just didn't take *time*. About five minutes to do everything assigned, and then I could get back to my music. I have to admit I could get used to that."

"I wouldn't if I were you," I said.

"Joking, joking."

That left an uncomfortable silence, and then I added to the awkwardness by saying, "So what else did he help you with?"

"Got me to my band practice an hour away," Devon said. "I was going to take the bus but he moved me there in the space of a heartbeat. Pretty cool."

"Public transit is cool, too," I said. "Extremely cool." The demon's favors were worrying me.

"Um, right," said Devon. "Well. I was there an hour early, so I had time to work on the new song."

"The butter one?"

He laughed. "You have to remember, we've been playing a lot of schools and churches," he said. "Emo songs don't make it

past the review committees. So far this year I've written one
song about Saturday afternoons at the dog park, one about uni-
cycling giraffes, and one about a mopey Batman in love with
Superman. Well, that one is kind of emo. Anyway, this one isn't
about superheroes or giraffes or anything else. It's simply about
a girl." His voice dropped down into that velvety thing it does
when he's singing.

"Is that so?" I managed.

"A plain ordinary girl."

"Oh."

"Well, maybe not very plain at all."

"Oh?"

"And maybe not very ordinary in the slightest."

"Tell me more."

"It was going to be about a girl who tamed demons, but demons never make it past the censors."

"So what does this not very plain, not very ordinary girl do?"

He sang, soft and in my ear.

"She's a cool stick of butter
  With a warm warm heart
  The Serengeti loves her
  'Cause she takes their part

  She shoulders up her tranqs
  To put the humans down
  She stands with the lions
  The bad guys hit the ground

  She's a lion tamer, a lion tamer
  And she's on their side
  She's a lion tamer, a lion tamer
  And she's one of their pride

When she finds me at the bus stop
I'm a loner with a mane
The world wants to cage me
'Cause they think I am insane

But she shoulders up her tranqs
To put the whole world down
She stands next to me
When the bad guys come around

She's a lion tamer, a lion tamer
She's on my side
She's a lion tamer, a lion tamer
And I'm one of her pride.

"Good night, Cam," he said.

"Good night," I whispered back.

Homework not done. Spellbooks not researched. I had to be up at five-thirty for my regular chores.

But oh . . . my silly, fluttery heart made it hard to care.

I set the alarm an hour early and plunged into lovely demon-free dreams.

In the morning, it was pouring rain. The garage was leaking onto Moonfire, sizzling where it hit her scales. I ran around nailing tarps and stacking up pans, and my extra hour didn't buy me a bit of time. When I finally got to the ten minutes I was supposed to spend on deciphering that spell for self-defense, my mind was elsewhere.

I suppose that's why, when I looked down at my sheet of scratch paper, I realized I had started by carefully writing out the list of things I knew.

"Hells," I breathed. Spells really *were* just like a big word problem.

I studied the spell further. It certainly wasn't like any algebra problem I'd worked last night, because of all that stuff about ingredients higher than nine starting with *P* and so on. But if you considered that that part was like a logic problem . . . and that other parts were like crosswords or anagrams . . . I started lining up the things I knew about the ingredients. Turning them into equations. Crossing off things as soon as I knew I didn't need them.

And then I had it.

Two and a half tablespoons chopped pear, two tablespoons water, three tablespoons maple syrup, and one pinch each pepper and paprika. The only necessary gesture was to make sure you chopped the pears with both hands. It even sounded tasty.

The witch had said it was a beginner's spell, and I'd never believed her.

Now that I'd figured it out, I almost wanted to try it. But the bus was already coming down the street. I stuffed the self-defense spell and the witch's books in my backpack, and ran through the rain to the bus stop.

"Almost didn't make it," said Oliver as I climbed aboard.

"Then you wouldn't have this," I said, and handed him a tiny mister for his windshield.

"Whatta girl," said Oliver as he accelerated. "I'll put it on soon as I make up the time I lost. That stuff's magic."

"Yup," I said. I wiped rain from my frizzing hair, looking over his shoulder for Devon. After last night, I was dying to see him in person. To see what his face would reveal when he saw me. But yet again, no Devon on the bus. I hoped the demon wasn't making him walk the four miles to school in the pouring rain.

"I already saw your friend this morning," Oliver said. "He got on when I swung through here an hour ago."

I looked quizzically at him.

"You know, your friend that poured water on my nice dry bus," he said. "I saw him."

"How'd he look?"

"Dry," said Oliver. "I particularly noticed that. Everyone else looked like they'd been through a car wash, but not him. I almost didn't recognize him. You know I recognize people by the tops of their heads as they come up the stairs, and now his hair's changed color . . ."

"Thanks, Oliver," I said. "You ever stop driving buses, you can take up a career in espionage."

"Espionage," he said, trying out the sound of it. "Double-O-Oliver."

No Devon on the bus, no Devon by the dripping-wet T-Bird, and certainly no Devon by my locker in the tenth-grade wing. Demons made it hard to have a smooth social life.

But a group of girls was clustered around a dim blonde and a black-haired girl in sparkly black, and when they saw me, the snickers erupted. I ignored that, because obviously when someone looks at you and snickers, it is on purpose to be superannoying. I concentrated on toweling my hair with my hoodie as I went past.

I got along well enough with those girls when they weren't under Sparkle's influence—as in, we weren't BFFs, but we were friendly enough. I knew one from biology, a couple from grade school, and I'd shared a laugh or two with all of them at one point.

So whatever their deal was today, I refused to play those Sparkle-driven games. I tied my damp hoodie around my waist and opened my locker.

"Was it second base?" said Reese.

Go back four places and lose one turn. "What did you say?"

"Don't play dumb, Camellia," said Reese. I should have been

alerted by the open hostility in her tone. "We all know you were on the rooftop making out with Devon after school."

And then, the double whammy.

"How's it feel to be left for someone more popular?"

11

Who Was Where with Whom

Shock waves ran through me at the implications of that last sentence, and then, backing up, for the flat-out horrid feeling of being accused. Ten girls surrounding you and laughing about *something you did* will have that effect on you, no matter what the something or how true it was.

Fumbling, I said: "I was not." My policy of ignoring Sparkle's girls when they were obnoxious was suddenly in shreds. Everything was in shreds. I was splayed open in a crowded green-painted hallway while a group of miniskirted tigers circled, watching to see what I'd do.

"You don't know what you're talking about," I said, dumping textbooks in my locker.

Reese's eyes narrowed. "Got it from the source."

The source? The only other person who'd been there was—"You!" I rounded on Sparkle.

Sparkle laughed in my face, black hair tumbling. "I didn't say one word," she said.

"Liar," I said. "You know perfectly well what I've got here." I tugged my phone from my damp jeans pocket.

"Not a clue," said Sparkle. I saw her glance behind me but I was too late. Three girls slammed into me. My phone squeezed from my fingers, banged to the floor. Another girl grabbed it and tossed it to Sparkle.

I felt my wrist where someone's shoulder had crunched it.

I was going to be a mass of bruises by Halloween. "Wow, way to ambush me with lies," I said. "Bravo."

Sparkle smirked. "I'm not the idiot who was snuggling with a boy on a rooftop in broad daylight," she said. "You know how rumor spreads. I didn't have to say anything." She pressed buttons on the phone, which apparently had turned off again. "How do you get this thing on?"

"You could've said it wasn't true," I muttered, even though that made me feel all mixed up inside because of course I wished it was. How is it that you could want two completely opposite things to happen? I didn't want this scene to happen, where a gaggle of Sparkle's minions accused me of kissing Devon . . . but of course I would've liked to have kissed Devon. And would've much rather had that happen than what *did* happen on the rooftop. Even if it meant the teasing would be true.

"What's wrong with your stupid phone?" said Sparkle.

"You dropped it," I said calmly. "Congratulations."

Reese was standing off to the side, eyeing me. She looked half-sad, half like she would like to gouge my eyes out with her manicure.

"Devon and I didn't do anything," I offered. "This was just a setup by Sparkle to get my cell phone and you know it."

But Reese in love was not-nice Reese. She stabbed a finger into my shoulder. "He's *my* crush," she said. "I'm paying for him. You'd better back off."

"Or what. You'll poke me to death?" Several of Sparkle's girls giggled at that. They wouldn't have sided with me against Sparkle, of course, but I was irrationally heartened to know they would against dim-bulb Reese.

"Oh, take your stupid brick," said Sparkle, and she shoved the phone into my chest.

"Thanks, chum," I said. "Catch ya later, girls. This was fun.

Let's do it again sometime." I ignored the fuming blond chick an inch from me.

Several girls grabbed Reese and pulled. "C'mon. Crane's coming."

Reese sent one more parting shot: "At least he met me in public."

Reese. He'd met *Reese*? I was dying to know what they were talking about, but damned if I'd ask. "Where was that? The petting zoo?"

Sparkle smiled nastily. "Wouldn't you like to know what he does when he's not with you?"

The other girls laughed again as they tugged Reese off. Sparkle slipped through and to the front of the pack, marching them off to class or further mischief or wherever. Her black hair swung against her relatively subdued black beaded dress.

"That was interesting," said Jenah behind me.

"You saw?"

"Not live and in person, but Elly Sinclair got a blurry video, and then Barry sent me three texts about it." She tested the air with a finger. "Of course, it's obvious from the disturbances in the hallway that some girl-girl altercation went down. And way to play into stereotypes, girls! It was about a boy."

I groaned and tugged on my damp hair. "Why didn't I think on the spot? I should've laughed and said something like, 'Of course we were making out on the roof. It was awesome.' That would've stopped them. And what did Reese mean by meeting him in public? Tell me. Do you know?"

"You aren't going to like it," said Jenah. "Francie told me that Ellen saw Reese and Devon at Blue Moon Pizza together last night. They were holding hands over the cheese sticks."

"Last night. Last night while I was worrying about him? While I was obsessing to you about how I could rescue him from Estahoth? *That* last night?"

"They didn't kiss, if that's any consolation. Francie said Reese kept trying to scoot in and tilt her lips into prime kissing position, but he blocked her. Checked her with his shoulder."

"I didn't get my English homework read because I was talking to him on the phone. He did not say one word."

Jenah looked at me like, duh, of course he wouldn't. "So *were* you making out on the roof?" she said. "Because we're sharing everything now, you know."

That made me laugh, despite the horrid shamed feeling. "No, we didn't." I pondered. "I guess he must've just flat out told Reese about the rooftop. How obnoxious. Because I could see some people in the park, but they were pretty far away, and they wouldn't have known who we were, even *if* they saw us. Not that there was anything to see, because nothing happened."

Jenah pursed her lips. "Okay."

"Okay, what?"

"Okay, maybe I believe you." She said that matter-of-factly, like she was keeping me up-to-date on the situation.

"Hells, Jenah. I never lied to you about anything but the witch, and I just couldn't tell anyone about that. What?"

"You didn't tell me any of this roof stuff."

I didn't? I scoured my memory. "Ack," I said. "Only because I got derailed by Sparkle's nose, and then you interrupted to say that—" I lowered my voice—"Moonfire was talking to you." And maybe also because the memory of poor Devon forced to destroy those pixies was so horrible that deep down, I hadn't wanted to talk about it.

Crap.

I'd always thought of myself as honest. Why was my subconscious working against me? Why were some things so difficult to push past your lips?

"So I left Sparkle, and went into the auditorium—" I said.

"But first, you saw me," said Jenah. She smoothed her filmy green skirt over her black leggings.

I endured the embarrassment. "Yes. I saw you. I'm sorry. And then I found Devon on the roof with the box you saw yesterday . . ." In a couple sentences I outlined the rest of that horror.

"Oh," said Jenah. She swallowed. "Magic isn't all fluffy butter-flies, is it?"

"No. But please. I am telling you the truth. As quickly as I can. So bear with me."

"I know," Jenah said. She patted my shoulder a couple times. "Look, we're going to be late to algebra. We better go."

So that was like ice in my gut. Jenah did trust me and she didn't, all at once. The frustrating thing was that her caution was, logically, the right thing. I could tell she wasn't just trying to piss me off, trying to get back at me. She would try to take me at my word, but she wasn't necessarily going to believe 100 percent of everything I said until she'd proven it for herself. Or maybe till great oceans of time passed and we were old and gray, or at least in college.

How the heck did I deal with that?

No Devon in algebra, and you'll think I'm an idiot, but I slid the demon book into my binder and studied it instead of alge-bra. Okay, so I'm an idiot. But I had one day to put a spell to-gether, and that meant I needed lunch today to gather any ingredients I might need.

I found the part about pentagrams straight off, and the good news there was that the spell didn't need anything besides the pentagram itself, one breath from the witch, and the touch of her wand. It wasn't even written in code, either. I guess because it was so straightforward—and so important. Besides demon-summoning, pentagrams could also contain witches, humans—even phoenix and dragons. The only catch for using a pentagram as a jail was that you had to get the entity inside first.

Some catch.

Still, it was the only plan I had. And the fact that a pentagram wasn't much of a spell meant I really only had to figure out one spell, the big spell, the tremendous spell.

A spell to get the demon out of Devon.

If such a spell even existed.

I skimmed pages, looking. There were several pages of different summoning spells, and I thought I recognized the one the witch used, with the basil and salamander. Then several pages of how to lock demons into bodies. Was getting the demon up to Earth all that witches cared about? How could the book have pages and pages of how to get a demon here, but nothing about controlling your demon once you've got him? Nothing about damage control? I supposed because demons couldn't get into *witches* unless they let them in, they didn't give two hoots for the regular humans in danger. Typical.

On the very last page I found the spell I sought.

The title was: *Ye Olde Demon-Loosening Spell for Feeble-minded Witches Who Have Changed Their Minds About Which Puny Human Should Hold Said Demon.*

Then there were the caveats, a whole bunch of "We've heard this works, but the demon had already gotten himself embodied so that's probably why it failed," and, "We've heard this works, but the witch disappeared and so did the demon."

Yeah.

We've heard this works but—help, help, I'm being eaten, I thought sourly.

There was a list of ten ingredients and then the complex

instructions, as usual. I didn't have time to attempt to "solve" the recipe and see which ingredients were needed and which weren't.

Hastily I scribbled them all on a sheet of torn-out notebook paper. Three of them were grocery items we didn't have at home: eggplant, oysters, apples. One of the ingredients was goat's blood. I sighed. Why didn't the witch just keep a goshdarn goat, if it was going to be this important? I scanned the complex directions and saw immediately that the required amount of goat's blood was one ounce and the number of apples was two. But I was going to have to decipher the rest of the spell to see how much of the other items I needed.

So I'd go to Celestial Foods and get the grocery items, plus the stuff off the list Sarmine had left out for me. After a moment's thought I added pears and maple syrup to the list, for the self-defense spell. The bell rang and I scrambled up.

"Camellia? Up here a moment."

Hells.

Well, I wasn't going to break down for Rourke. If he was still mad from yesterday, he was still mad.

But Rourke, oddly enough, was smiling. I suppose he liked delivering bad news.

"I talked to your aunt last night," he said. "She was kind enough to stop by."

"Crap, you saw her?" Rourke frowned. "Er. Sorry. I mean, I figured you would've gone home. How late do you stay here?" I didn't say, Don't you have a life? but I was thinking it, along with, WITCH HERE WITCH HERE OMG OMG.

His eyebrows merged quizzically. "Football practice? I'm the assistant coach."

Pride absolutely suffocated his voice, so I managed, "Of course! I knew that. We've got a great team, really great."

"Your aunt watched the entire practice. She was really

enthusiastic. Kept asking me all sorts of questions about the school's history."

"Mmm," I said.

"Look. The point is we'll try this once more tonight. Your aunt pled your case, and against all odds, your tutor pled your case," said Rourke. "Your aunt said you had been busy of late helping her out on a project. She is quite charming, you know. Why haven't we seen her around here more often?"

"She's been in Nepal. She's not that charming once you get to know her. She's busy trying to overthrow the government. She's shy. She's frightened. She's frightening."

Visible Undershirt actually laughed. "I see where you get your sense of humor," he said. "Well, tell your aunt I look forward to seeing her tomorrow."

"Righto. And why will you be doing that?" If Visible Undershirt had asked Sarmine out on a date, I'd never live it down. He must be really lonely to even think of it. And where would he take her? I guarantee you there was no restaurant in town that served both two-liters of root beer and roc eggs on toast points. I could only think of one thing worse than the two of them dating, and that was . . .

"She was interested in being a school parent for the Halloween Dance," he said. "I sent her over to Miss Crane to sign up. I expect she'll be delightful company."

Crap.

Crap.

Crap.

"I expect," I said.

I am normally very organized, but events this week had gotten a little out of hand. I made a list in English class while everyone else read out loud from the play.

- Solve Ye Olde Demon-Loosening Spell (MOST IM-PORTANT)
- Get demon-loosening ingredients and self-defense ingredients
- Retake algebra test
- Figure out how the demon is planning to steal "the hopes and dreams of five"
- Figure out why Devon is hanging out with Reese and her blue bra

In a bleak moment I thought that no matter how many of those things I managed successfully, it didn't matter, because the witch was going to show up at the dance on Friday and make whatever social life I had left a living hell. After my classmates found out I lived with somebody who chanted nonsense words and wore a fanny pack full of spices and, oh yeah, *hexed people* every time they looked at her wrong, my life would be shot. It would be worse than ten girls teasing me one day about a boy and forgetting about it the next. The humiliation would never end.

And now I was going to try a spell, which I'd sworn I'd never do.

As you can see, I was a little overwhelmed at this point. I'd gone my whole life managing to handle everything the witch threw at me. Fulfill crazy-ass demands for eel and unicorn hairs and puréed Chinese gooseberries. Juggle home life and school life and keep the two completely separate, one never intruding on the other.

I guess this time I was just in over my head.

But still, I knew deep down that taking a step toward evil witchdom was worth the risk to save Devon. And not just because I liked him, either.

Because it was *right*.

I was still stressed about it, though.

I desperately wanted to find Devon at lunch and find out if the story about Reese was true, but instead I set off for Celestial Foods. No matter how many fluttering doubts were building up inside me, I was going to stick to my plan. If I *could* work spells, then I was going to get that demon out of Devon and nothing was going to stop me.

I hurried out the side door, past the metal T-Bird, jumped over the little mouse. I had tripped on the mouse sculpture once and gone sprawling into a total make-out session. I swear, the school has this ivy and stuff pruned all the time to cut down on people sneaking over here, but it seems to grow back overnight. So I avoided the mouse and two different couples, but then my foot slid on the wet leaves and my next step took me into the bushes and sprawling over a leg.

A leg attached to a boy who stood up hastily out of the shadow of the overgrown bushes.

A boy I recognized.

A boy-band boy.

"Are you all right?" I said before I thought. "I was worried about you." Then my face fell. How much was he hiding from me . . . and who was standing in front of me, hiding it?

I peered into kind green eyes, searching. Devon smiled the typical Devon shy smile and I was instantly relieved. "Don't worry," he said. "I'm doing much better." He brushed wet leaves from his shirt.

"I was worried when I didn't see you in algebra," I said. And then forthright me just had to say it: "Look, I heard you were out having pizza with Reese last night. I mean, it's none of my business, but I guess I was curious because you said you were at your band practice? Was that some sort of Estahoth-related thing, maybe?" Sure, I had reason to find out what the demon was up to, but the question came out all weak-sounding and I hated it.

"Yeah, Estahoth made a hologram of me while I was at band practice," he said. "He was working on the tasks."

"Ah. Cool," I said. There was so much relief at that, that I didn't want to acknowledge the niggling question in my head that said—why on earth was the demon taking Reese to pizza as part of a task? "Well, you're looking tons better. Which is great. Because like he said yesterday, he's here till Halloween anyway. Tomorrow. And . . . well, I guess he can hear or remember everything we say—Hi, Esty-snookums—so there are certain topics I'm not going to go into." I was dying to tell Devon of my plan to trap him in a pentagram, but obviously that would be the dumbest idea ever.

"Er. That's probably good," he said.

"Yeah." I knew I should get going to get the ingredients, but you know how it is when you run into your crush. And fine, I admit it, the shy boy-band boy was becoming more and more my crush every time we talked. Which is why I was so glad that the thing with Reese wasn't a real thing. You know how it sucks when you like something for its inner essence but then everyone else likes it for its superficial outer stuff? And you want to say, "But *I'm* not following the herd," and *then* you feel like some sort of fakey hipster? That's how I felt about falling for Devon. If he was a boy-band boy, then he was my personal obscure boy-band boy, and I wanted him to stay that way.

"So . . . what about task three?" I said. "I think we might have to help Mr. Esty fill that one regardless."

Devon shifted and kinda looked down at the bushes and back. "Why?"

"Because the, um, 'woman' says the, um, 'bird' is going to explode no matter what," I said, quotation marking the substitutions for all I was worth. "And I think she's telling the truth with this one. That energy has to go somewhere, and having it burst into flame on the school grounds would be . . . pretty awful. So it has to be found, and probably harnessed, because we can't get old Rabby up to a barren mountaintop in time."

Devon was looking at the bushes again. "Are you really doing okay? Is there someone back there?"

He looked up at me. "I'm going to make it to tomorrow. You don't have to worry about me."

"Good," I said. He looked kinda shifty, but I suppose it probably was taking a lot of control to keep the demon suppressed and their personalities nice and separate, no matter how slick he claimed it was going. "So what was the trick?"

"No trick," said Devon. "We're just sort of coexisting. It's going great." His hair flopped forward.

His black hair.

"Wait a minute," I said. "Your hair's still black."

"I like it that way?"

"It usually changes when you're *you*." I peered closer. "Is that lip gloss on your cheek?" I tried to laugh. "I mean, I know the demon likes changing colors, but surely he didn't decide it would be cool to have a shimmery pink smear half on and off your ear."

"Camellia," he said formally. "Do you know Reese?"

12

Zombie Girl

A wobbly blond girl wobbled up from the bushes. "He kissed me," Reese said dreamily.

"*Really*," I said.

"Mmmmm," said Reese.

"But you just said you were Devon," I said.

"Right," Devon said, and smirked.

"Kissed me, kissed me," said Reese. Her eyes crossed.

"I don't know who you are anymore," I said. "If you're the demon, then you've gotten really good at imitating Devon. If you're Devon, then . . ."

"Kissed me," said Reese.

"Okay, what's wrong with her?" I said.

Devon patted her shoulder. "It's time to be quiet. Think quiet thoughts."

Reese swung around and looked vaguely off in the distance. She waved at a cloud. It was freaky, like she was some sort of zombie girl under the demon's spell. But why would the demon need a zombie-girl minion? And then I realized that he didn't.

The witch did.

"Holy hells," I said. "Reese? What's your name? What's two plus two?"

Reese looked slyly at me. She mimed zipping up her lips and shook her head. She made kissy faces at the cloud.

"Squishing pixies, finding the phoenix, and *collecting hopes and dreams,"* I said to Devon/Estahoth. "This is what happens when you take her hopes and dreams?"

"Kinda sucks, huh?" he said. "You think people are going to notice?"

"Um. Yeah," I said. Reese took Devon's arm and kissed his shoulder. He patted her head. "Yeah, I think people are going to notice. I think lots and lots of people are going to notice."

"Sit down," Devon told Reese. "Pat the mousey statue."

Reese fed it ivy and whispered, "Kissed me, kissed me," to it. There were grass stains all over her white T-shirt. The damp spots showed that today her bra was orange, which was just totally annoying. The smell of the wet ivy drifted up from the damp earth. Or was that mold and firecrackers?

"So you were lying before," I said. "I mean *Estahoth. You* were lying."

"About which thing?"

I ignored that, because the demon was obviously trying to provoke me, just like Sparkle's girls had been. "When you told Devon you didn't have powers while you were inside him."

"Oh, that," said Estahoth. "No, I didn't at first. But I have them now that Devon is sharing more and more with me. We tried them out last night. We're trusting each other now, and I'm learning how I can help him." He smiled wryly at me. "I know I was kind of a jerk at first."

"Kind of!"

"But think of my disadvantaged background! Stuck in the fires of the Earth, able to learn only little snippets about life on Earth from those who went up and came back. You know, it's a pretty funny sight, now that I think about it. All the demons sitting around, waiting for whoever was called to come back and tell us every detail. One demon told us all about Elvis. We all practiced shaking our pelvises after that. Well, in our imaginations we did," he amended. "Demons don't normally have pelvises."

"How many times have you been up here?" I said.

"Three," he said, and there was something venomous in his tone. "I almost had it the second time. Sixteen ninety-two, Massachusetts. I almost made it."

Involuntarily I took a step backward. "If you'd made it *then*, you'd be dead by now," I said. "Isn't that the catch?"

"But I would've *lived*," he said. He seemed to notice my expression and plastered a grin back on his face. "But you're right. I wouldn't be here helping Devon. He gets to kiss five girls, I get to suck away their 'hopes and dreams' to fulfill my contract. Win-win. And this is a glorious little spot of history you're in."

"You are *not* helping him," I said. "And why did you set it up so kissing a girl is the way to work the spell?"

"To reward him, of course."

"He doesn't want your rewards. Does he?"

The demon grinned. "Here, we'll ask him. I'm not trying to suppress him, you know. We're friends now. Hey, ask him if he wants to go as Elvis for Halloween tomorrow. I think I could really get the moves right."

The demon shook his head—and his pelvis—until he blinked and spoke in a different tone. A different tone, but the same hair color, the same stance. It was getting harder and harder to tell when the two of them shifted—or if any of the shifts were real.

"It's not a reward, Cam," he said earnestly. "I don't want to kiss five girls."

"Oh, please," I said. "Be reasonable. Who wouldn't?" The words came out more sarcastic than broad-minded.

Devon stepped over Reese's muddy legs and took my hand. Electric fire tingled up my hand and I almost jerked away. "Really," he said. "I'm just playing along to make it out of this alive.

I wouldn't have ended up in the bushes with Reese on purpose. Reese is a nice girl, but a little . . ."

"Kissed me?" Reese suggested.

"Repetitive," Devon said.

I laughed and he pulled me closer.

"I want you to go to the dance with me tomorrow," he said.

"To be there if you need help, you mean," I said.

"No, to go with me. To be my date. You," he said.

"I could go for that," I said, heart bursting into song and sunshine.

"I'll show you that there's only one girl I want to kiss," he said, smoothly, calmly, delightfully.

I melted, melted—and then—hells! I stuck my hand straight out and stopped him an inch from my lips. Shoved him backward. He stumbled against the mock-orange bush. "I am so not your little idiot," I said. But I almost had been.

Whoever he was, he waggled his fingers and grinned cheekily at me. "Four more to go," he said.

I booked it to Celestial Foods. Grabbed the ever-growing list of ingredients for various spells off the metal shelves, panting. I had no idea how many oysters or eggplant the demon-loosening spell needed so I grabbed a tin of the former and ten of the latter. I desperately wanted a new jar of peanut butter so I could eat some lunch, but I didn't have enough change. As it was I had to put one of the eggplants back.

"Another trip for your aunt?" said Celeste. Her wooden hippie necklaces clacked reassuringly as she leaned over to scan my produce. It was a homey sound.

"The weary grind never ceases," I joked.

Celeste studied the display screen while sliding my grocery items across her scanner. "I suppose things change all the time," she said casually. "You know, back when Alphonse was at Hal Headley they had half an hour lunch breaks."

"Oh?" I said. I had no idea where she was going with this.

"Well, you know my boy. He's always been an activist, always taking up someone's cause. At that time they didn't have a vegetarian option in the cafeteria, except for a pathetic salad bar containing wilted lettuce and soggy veg. Can you imagine?" She shook her head, graying ringlets bobbing.

"No," I said. "They've got several options now. Every day."

"That's all Alphonse," Celeste said proudly. "He didn't have all sorts of time, because he helped me after school for an hour and a half each day, and he had his homework. So he had to balance school and helping his mum just like you do. But he took part of his lunch break every single day to work on it. He researched what other cafeterias across the States were doing. He took polls of students. He blogged about it. He made friends with the cafeteria workers and got their input. It was nobody's idea but his own. It was something he was passionate about and he spent all his spare time doing it."

"That's cool," I said. I didn't know what she was getting at but I liked hearing stories of her family. "Go Alphonse."

Celeste handed me my bag of ingredients. "I hope your aunt appreciates everything you do for her," she said.

I barely made it to American history and yet another scintillating video. I tuned out and tried to decipher what Celeste was trying to say with her Alphonse anecdote. That she appreciated him? That she let him live his own life? Certainly she thought the world of Alphonse, even when they disagreed. I knew she hated the dangerous tactics he and his friends used. She was terrified that he would come to harm. But at the same time she was proud of him for standing up for his beliefs. It must be hard to be a mom in those gray situations, where nothing was black-and-white, and nobody was 100 percent right or 100 percent wrong.

I didn't know. It was so hard to concentrate on anything without lunch. I was so hungry I was seriously starting to think about eating the spell ingredients.

By gym I was so desperate for food that I ate an airline cracker pack I found squashed at the bottom of my backpack. I shoved my feet into my gym shorts and hurried out to see if Zombie Reese had made it to gym class.

Reese was cross-eyed, but she was there. We were still doing track, so even Zombie Reese could handle a slow jog around the track, telling all her friends, "He kissed me." They swooned.

I guess I was wrong that people would notice.

Reese jogged next to me for a while in happy cross-eyed silence. I'd been pissed at her this morning, but it's impossible to be angry at a blissful zombie. At least she'd been taken in by a punk-band demon and not a pelvis-shaking demon.

"Soooo. How're the plans for the dance going?" I said through my panting. "The Halloween Dance Committee has everything under control?"

"Dunno," Reese said.

"Blue Crush still the band of choice?" I said.

"That's Devon's band," she said.

"I know," I said. It was hard to talk to zombies. "What do you want to do with your life?"

"Kiss Devon," she said.

That sounded like a hope and a dream to me, if a dumb one. "Do you remember what you used to want to do?" I said.

Reese looked up at the sky and stumbled a bit. "Um," she said. "Be a kindergarten teacher?"

"But now?"

"Kiss Devon," she said firmly.

"I hear you," I said.

"You want to kiss Devon, too?"

"Look, have you thought about this?" I said. "Maybe what you think you want isn't really what you want. Maybe what you want is just someone else telling you that that's what you want. And what you *really* want is buried so deep that it's hard to figure it out. You can barely remember what you want, because other people's needs and wants are so squashed on top of it."

"They are?"

I wiped sweat from my forehead. "You spend all your life reacting to what this other person wants of you," I said. The words bubbled up from the deep, a carbonated explosion. "Fulfilling their needs and helping them, or stopping them, but either way it's all about *them*. When is it going to be about you? *You've* got to ask the questions in life. *New* questions. 'Where are *my* hopes and dreams?' Do you know what I mean, Reese?" The words tore through and out of me until I felt empty, exhausted with the effort.

Or maybe that was the jogging.

"That cloud looks like Devon," said Reese.

I stopped dead in the path and grabbed her shoulder. "Is that him down there?"

Reese squealed and ran down the hill in the direction I'd pointed. There was a boy at the bottom of the hill with a younger girl, one I didn't know. I hurried behind Reese as she plowed down the hill and smacked full stop into Devon, wrapping her arms around him. I skidded on the wet grass and almost fell into both of them, but I stumbled back against the side of the hill instead, muddying my butt and hands.

The other girl reeled away. Her eyes were crossed.

"He kissed me," she said.

"He kissed you?" said Reese.

"He kissed me," said the other girl.

This could get tedious. "Reese, you need to finish jogging," I said. I tried to brush off my gym shorts but the mud and grass smeared the shiny polyester. "And you, what class should you be in right now?"

"Computer Programming Three," the girl said.

"So you like software?" I said. "You want to be a hacker? You're clever with code? It's your whole life, right? All the hopes and dreams you have are centered around computers?"

"I like him," she said. "He kissed me."

"Yes, we know. Both of you, scoot." I pried Reese from Devon and shoved both girls up the hill. Luckily, they didn't seemed inclined to fight. I just heard them informing each other that they'd been kissed as they wobbled up the hill.

I turned back to Devon, but he was gone. Vanished, and I think literally. All that was left was an echo of a voice saying, "Two down."

Hells.

I trudged up the steep slope to the end of gym class and the showers. What was I supposed to do, quarantine all the girls in school until I could get Devon into a pentagram? I pulled my list out of my backpack and made some notes.

- Solve Ye Olde Demon-Loosening Spell (MOST IM-PORTANT)*****
- ~~Get demon-loosening ingredients and self-defense ingredients~~
- Retake algebra test
- ~~Figure out how the demon is planning to steal "the hopes and dreams of five"~~
- ~~Figure out why Devon is hanging out with Reese and her blue bra~~
- Trap Devon in a pentagram

Well, there was one thing I could do now. When the bell rang, I crammed my muddy gym clothes in my bag, went straight to Rourke's classroom, and laid it out for him.

"Mr. Rourke," I said. "About the test I bombed . . . ?"

"Work your session with my tutor this afternoon and I'll let you retake it tomorrow. This once. And don't think you're getting away with anything. I know you were an A student in math last year, so I assume there's hope for you." Rourke chugged the last of a two-liter and tossed the bottle in the trash can.

"Right." I twisted my fingers and wondered if it would've done any good to buy Rourke a bottle of root beer. "So Kelvin's a really good tutor. After he explained it yesterday I really got it. I went home and worked." A few problems plus a self-defense spell was work. "I may be a bit slow, but . . . I'd like to take that test now." The thought made me nervous, but I hoped my show of confidence would convince Rourke to let me get this situation over with.

"Right now," said Rourke. "*Really.*" He grabbed another two-liter and thoughtfully twisted the cap back and forth, loosening it in tiny *crack-crack*s. "This would be your only chance."

"Once you understand that algebra's logical, then it's just working through the steps," I said. "Even with word problems."

"A plodding approach, but true enough," conceded Visible Undershirt. "All right then. Your gumption hurts no one but yourself."

Rourke handed me a new test from a locked drawer and I sat down at my desk. There was a moment of panic—why did I think this would be a good idea?—but then I stopped. Swallowed.

Compared to a self-defense spell written by a paranoid witch who added in seven extra ingredients and used jokes about body parts to solve steps, algebra was nothing.

Step.

By.

Step.

❮

I didn't get 100 percent, though probably if I were a boy-free nun on a witch-free island with three days to take the test, I could have. There was one problem where I suddenly forgot how to add exponents, and another where I added six and seven and got eleven. As you do. Long and short of it, I got a 91 percent. I was bummed when Rourke said he was going to average it with my 61 percent, but then he didn't completely. He gave me an 81 percent and said next time to ask for the tutor before I got behind. Then he offered me a celebratory root beer in a paper cup.

When I went out into the hallway, swigging my root beer, Kelvin was standing stiffly across the hall, watching Rourke's door. He was in his trench coat and it made him look like a poker-faced giant.

"Kelvin!" I said. "You're seriously the best. I got an A."

"I was only the catalyst to remind you that you could do it," Kelvin said. "The Post-it note on the refrigerator of your brain."

"Step. By. Step," I said. I slugged his arm. "You should totally become a math teacher. You got the chops and you'll have all the root beer you can drink."

"Mmm, root beer and chops," said Kelvin.

"Okay, look," I said. "I have one more favor to ask you. I'll pay you the usual and I don't need it till tomorrow, but it absolutely truly has to be goat's and not cow's blood. Can I get one ounce from you?"

Kelvin swallowed, Adam's apple bobbing into his trench collar. He closed his eyes and he said, "Will you go to the dance with me?"

My heart sunk into my belly.

Looking back, I guess I should've known.

I should've known, right? You probably saw it coming a mile off. But I had no idea. When you're focused on another boy, this kind of thing happens.

And then you feel awful.

"Kelvin . . ." I said. "I can't. I'm sorry."

His eyes were still closed. "Then no goat's blood."

I touched his arm and he flinched. "You don't really want to trade a dance for goat's blood, do you?"

Kelvin opened his eyes and deadpan he said, "It's fitting for a Halloween dance."

I couldn't tell if he was serious or not. "I'm kinda going with someone else," I said.

"Who?"

"Devon."

"The one who's been kissing all those girls?" he said.

"Well. Yes. It's not entirely his fault."

Lines furrowed Kelvin's brow. "Love is not logical," he said in his robot voice.

"I think you're nice," I said, which I know is a totally unhelpful thing to say. "Maybe we could, um, eat lunch together some time. Please, can you get me the goat's blood, though? I really am desperate for it."

"Not desperate enough to break your date with Romeo Lothario Especialo." Kelvin shoved his hands in his trench pockets. "I'm tired of being the helpful guy."

"Now wait, I always pay you," I said. "That's not a favor, that's a business transaction. And how did I know you were Rourke's algebra tutor? That's something you must have volunteered for a whole month ago."

He didn't say anything to that, just looked at the tiled ceiling, lips set in a thin stubborn line. Fleetingly, I wondered if I'd let slip earlier in the school year that I was having algebra problems.

"Gah!" I said. "You want me to break my date? Fine, I'll break it. If that's the only way to get the supplies I need. But I think it's a lousy way to get a girl to go out with you."

His wide face kind of trembled and he looked too embarrassed to speak. He grabbed his backpack and lurched away from me. "You never know when I'm joking," he said in his robot voice. "World never knows. World not understand robot Kelvin."

"You were joking?" I said. I wasn't sure if it was really true, but I wanted to believe it. "Thank goodness. So we're cool and you'll bring the goat's blood?"

He backed down the hall. "No more goats. Goats die of pig flu. This transaction is finished."

"Kelvin!" I said.

But he turned and ran.

13

Kiss Me

This is what I did Thursday evening while all the other kids in my school did homework and watched TV and texted each other and practiced violin and wrote poems and goofed off and painted self-portraits and leveled up and played basketball and practiced their stand-up and stared cross-eyed at their ceiling saying, "He kissed me."

I combed the garden for one earwig and four dandelion roots.

What I first did in the afternoon was take care of Wulfie and Moonfire, and then I sat down to solve the demon-loosening spell. But as soon as I started copying out the list of things I knew, I saw at the bottom that if the dandelion root was used, it must be gathered before the sun went down. So back outside I went to grab it before the sun set.

Clearly the more practical way to be a witch was to be prepared. Have plenty of time to work out the spell before you need to actually use it. Otherwise your life was spent doing everything in tiny backtracking increments, taking five times as long as you should to accomplish a spell. I supposed powerful witches like Sarmine had a million spells memorized and wore a fanny pack full of essential ingredients.

Even if I worked any more spells after this week, which I wasn't going to, there was no way I was going to wear a fanny pack.

When I came back in with the earwig and dandelions, I stopped in the kitchen and grabbed the pepper and paprika.

No use understanding the self-defense spell if I didn't try to mix it up, right? That wasn't a slippery slope, just good common sense.

Once alone in my bedroom, I dug out the book with the spell for demon-loosening.

1. If directed elsewhere to use #9 or #3, these are the measurements: 1 oz of #9, 2 units of #3.

Okay, so looking at the ingredients list, that was one ounce of goat's blood (where the heck was I going to get it now?) and two apples. I'd already figured that out.

2. If it is a Monday, use 1 oz of #12 and 18 units of #7. Else not, unless the date of the month adds up to 5 or is divisible by 5.

Halloween was not a Monday, and thirty-one did not add up to five nor was it divisible by five. So I didn't need number 7—pumpkin (darn, one easy ingredient)—or number 12—basilisk urine (thank goodness). I worked my way up to step four, which had a riddle about an ingredient made up of chicken containers plus green leafy things, and I got stuck. What was a chicken container? A coop? A saucepan? There weren't any ingredients that sounded like a coop or a saucepan.

I shoved that spell aside and dug out the paper with the self-defense spell on it. Slippery slope, here we come. I rechecked my solution from that morning and came up with the same answer: two and a half tablespoons chopped pear, two tablespoons water, three tablespoons maple syrup, one pinch each pepper and paprika; chop the pears with both hands.

Breathe.

Try it.

I grabbed a pear from my paper Celestial Foods bag and attempted to chop it with both hands. The pear slid out from under my knife and rolled onto the carpet, gathering brown carpet fuzz on the sliver my knife had cut.

Well, I wasn't going to eat the spell. I wedged the pear between my feet and tried chopping again. This time I got a slice whacked off. Should have gotten riper pears. I laid the pear on its flat side and chopped again. This wasn't so bad, just awkward.

The witch opened the door and I threw my hoodie over my feet. "Don't you knock?"

"Since when?" Sarmine said. "I just want to make sure everything's ready for tomorrow night. Have you been keeping track of the demon?"

"He's got your first two tasks done," I said. I assumed he'd finished kissing all those girls by this point. "I dunno if he's found the phoenix."

"He will," the witch said. "Elementals can always sense other elementals. That's my least worry. In fact, this all should go very smoothly. By this time tomorrow night the city will be under my command. And then there will be changes."

"What sort of changes?" I casually wiped pear juice on my hoodie and tugged my backpack to cover the open spellbook.

"It will be a grand day for witches," said Sarmine. "We will no longer be oppressed. We can come out of hiding and show the world our talents. The recycling program will expand. All city engineers will be directed to work on alternative-fuel solutions. Solar panels for all."

"That actually sounds reasonable," I said.

"And the city shall do my bidding in all things."

"That, not so much."

"Camellia," said the witch. She squatted down by my backpack. I could see another of her spellbooks, the radio one, sticking out. I tried not to look over there. "Camellia, I'd like to talk to you."

What had I done wrong now? I twisted awkwardly with my feet still covered, and grabbed the bag from Celestial Foods. "I got the things you needed for your spell tomorrow," I said. "Ginger root, black-tea bags, apples, and rubber bands."

"Good," she said, and took the ingredients from me. She turned the ginger root over in her hands. Finally she said, "Have you thought any more about trying to work a spell?"

Eek. "I'm kinda busy with my schoolwork right now," I said.

She nodded, and her face was kind of soft and searching. "Sometime, perhaps. Still plodding along on that self-defense spell?"

"Still plodding," I said with fake cheerfulness.

Sarmine rose and looked around the room. It was a mess. Besides the random pile of nine eggplants and jar of earwig and so forth, the feathers from the pillow that Wulfie had shredded clung to the bedspread and the wall and covered the floor in drifts. Sarmine considered. "Do you have a piece of Scotch tape?" she said.

"Um. Yeah." I found her the dispenser. The witch gathered two feathers and dusted them with a red-brown powder from her fanny pack that smelled like cinnamon. "EhLARu," Sarmine said, and pointed at the pillow with her aluminum wand.

Feathers whisked off the floor and into the pillow. The cotton case rewove itself around Wulfie's rips and tears and stitched itself closed. "You like animals, don't you?" Sarmine said.

The scope of the question was like asking someone if she liked food. Nevertheless, I was amazed at this sign that she knew anything about me at all. "Yes."

The mended pillow plopped into the pillowcase, which rewove its own damage. "EhLARil, larIL," she said, and blew something off her fingertip at the case. A pattern of tiny green turtles embroidered itself along the edges. The pillow plopped down onto the head of the bed with a soft thump.

"Thank you," I stammered.

The witch nodded and left my room. "See you tomorrow night," she said.

I flung my hoodie aside and finished chopping the pear. Combined it with the syrup and water and spices and mixed them all in a plastic pencil box.

It looked like pie filling.

Maybe I'd managed to interpret spells, but that didn't mean I could work them. I dug under my bed for the wand I'd taken from the witch's study and pulled it out.

It was black wood with a white tip. I hoped the white tip wasn't ivory, because I would hate that. But when I looked closer it seemed to be made of that shimmery stuff that comes from seashells. The black wood felt solid, but I knew it couldn't be. All wands have to have something elemental in them, which in practice is usually dragon milk, dragon scales, or phoenix feather. I wondered if anyone had ever managed to make a wand with essence of demon in it. It seemed unlikely.

I hefted the wand in my hand. It was shorter and sturdier than the witch's wand. I liked the feel of it. It felt practical, and somehow warm, too.

I held it over the pencil box of pear mixture. What would a self-defense spell do if no one was attacking me? I dipped the tip of the wand into the pear.

Nothing.

"Because I'm not a witch," I growled, then stopped. If I was doing this because Jenah was right that maybe anyone could work spells, then I was going to have to go about this the right way. Spells required intention. Not me thinking, I'm not a witch.

"Even goats have magic in them," I said. "I'm practically a goat. I'm a goat, I'm a goat." I lowered the tip of the wand to the pear.

This time a shot like a bolt of electricity went up my arm. I jerked back, the wand flicking out just like the witch's always did—straight at the pyramid of nine eggplants.

The pyramid exploded.

Bits of eggplant covered my backpack, my desk, my ceiling. My bedspread. My new pillowcase with its tiny green turtles.

Despite the mess, I laughed hysterically. "Eggplant," I said. Chicken container plus green leafy thing. "Egg. Plant."

Friday morning. Halloween.

The school was buzzing with the holiday. Officially, the school prohibited costumes during the school day, but I saw lots of people with add-ons like kitten tails or nerd glasses. The Halloween Dance Committee whisked in and out of classes on "official" business. Rourke passed out gawdawful root beer candies.

Devon wasn't coming to classes anymore, but he was there at school, wandering all around and looking for the phoenix. In some ways that was the most important thing of the day, because if he didn't find it, the school would blow up. He didn't seem worried, though I suppose he expected he could teleport away or whatever if the phoenix blew. But the rest of us didn't have that luxury, and the idea of telling the principal to cancel the Halloween Dance because something in her school was going to blow up tonight would probably get me arrested on a bomb threat charge.

I couldn't concentrate on classes with everything jumping through my brain. I pulled out my list to see where we were:

- ~~Solve Ye Olde Demon-Loosening Spell (MOST IM-PORTANT)*****~~
- ~~Get demon-loosening ingredients and self-defense ingredients~~
- ~~Retake algebra test~~
- ~~Figure out how the demon is planning to steal "the hopes and dreams of five"~~
- ~~Figure out why Devon is hanging out with Reese and her blue bra~~
- Trap Devon in a pentagram
- Compound Demon-Loosening Spell (in progress!)
- Check and see if Devon has located the phoenix

My wand was in my backpack, along with Tupperwares full of ingredients. After I had had my eggplant breakthrough last night, I had started mixing the demon-loosening spell. By lunch the apple-oyster mixture had steeped for twelve hours, so I used part of lunchtime to stand at my locker and stir in earwigs and dandelions and so forth.

"Any luck?" I asked Jenah when I finally got to the cafeteria. I had put her in charge of identifying the five girls whom Devon had kissed. As far as I knew, the demon hadn't handed the "hopes and dreams" off to the witch—however one did that—so he must still have them all, somehow. Devon, plus a demon, plus the important parts of five girls—that poor boy was stuffed.

Jenah was sitting next to some girl whose head was cradled in her hands, obscuring her face. I plonked down whatever it was the lunch lady had handed me, and started scarfing it.

"Yes, in fact," Jenah said. "I've located all five zombie girls. The two you saw, plus Avery from the tennis team and *two* seniors."

"Wow. Moving up in the world." The girl next to Jenah had

limp blond hair that dragged in her lasagna, turning the ends tomato red. "Um, your hair . . ." I said.

Jenah gently shook the girl's shoulders. "Hey. Sit up," she said.

The blond girl shook her head, further moistening her hair.

Jenah pushed the girl's tray away, took her paper napkin, and began cleaning tomato off the girl's hair. "I was briefly distracted when I heard a rumor that he'd gotten *Miss Crane*," she said to me. "Can you imagine?"

Even in the middle of disaster I could see the funny side of that. "I would pay to see that."

"Apparently she'd gone to the dentist and *that's* why she was drooling," said Jenah. "It's been tricky sorting out who the girls are when no one knows the real story. But with little hints— this girl seemed high, that girl was singing 'Kiss Me' in the halls—I tracked all five of them down." She put the tomato-ey napkin back on the tray. "There you go, Reese."

The girl finally looked up at the sound of her name. Her eyes were dull and forlorn. I had not even recognized her. "He's all I want," Reese said.

"Oh, no," I said. "She's worse."

"It's like she needs her fix," Jenah said. "She was dreamy Reese before school. Said she saw him at his locker. Then he disappeared and won't answer her texts. Now she's like this."

"What do I do without him?" Reese said.

Despite knowing that the hope-stealing was magically induced, I tried reasoning with poor Reese. "Remember he's just a boy," I said. "He's not worth it. You have so many other things you want to accomplish."

Brief life snapped in Reese's eyes. "He's not *just* a boy and you know it."

Jenah and I exchanged a look, but we knew Reese didn't mean what we were thinking.

"Just a boy," I repeated. "No boy is worth giving up your *self* for."

Reese looked down at her tray and her lip trembled. "The lasagna looks like Devon," she said. Her hair tumbled back into her tray, covering her face. Jenah tried to sit her up, but she wouldn't budge.

"Add that to the list of tasks," I said. "We've got to reverse this horrible process before the witch gets ahold of their hopes and dreams and steals them for all time." Reese's state was so disturbing that I covered up my fear with flippancy. "I don't want to hear that she's seeing Devon in pieces of toast."

So Devon was definitely on my mind, but I didn't see him close up till just after lunch. Till just after the American history video about All Hallows' Eve got interrupted by a frog jumping out of nowhere.

A frog with wings that only I could see.

I jumped from my desk and grabbed the little thing out of the hair of a squealing girl.

"I think it escaped from Ms. Sanghvi's biology lab," I said. "I'll take it back to her."

Mrs. Taylor squeaked, "Just get it out of here."

So one pixie had escaped the rooftop massacre. To fulfill the witch's contract, the demon needed one hundred pixies at the school by Friday. It was Friday, so that was fulfilled. Now, if I could get this little guy *out* of the school, then that was one less pixie that the witch would have for her Ye Olde Becoming the Mayor Spell. Without all the ingredients, she couldn't take over the city, no matter whether I succeeded with my other plans or not.

I took the little pixie down the hall. It was a rich green color, speckled with tiny green dots like flecks of ash. It fluttered in my hand. I almost didn't see the pink flash that illuminated an empty classroom down the side hall.

I nudged open the door. "Devon?"

Devon was up on a table, running his fingers along the ceiling. "I know the phoenix is on the property," he said. "I can feel him. He's somewhere cold. But when he got put here fourteen years ago, he got loose from that demon and zoomed around the school first."

"What demon?"

Devon rolled his eyes at me. "Dragon, phoenix, and demon fell—"

"Yes, yes, I know," I said hastily. "You mean, that witch who transformed the phoenix, had to summon a demon to do it for her? Just like Sarmine did with you."

"Obviously."

"So really, the human is kind of like the wand," I said thoughtfully. "You can put dragon scales or phoenix feathers in a wand and use that, but to harness the power of demons you have to put them in a human. The human *is* the wand."

"I am not a wand," said Devon in a grouchy tone.

"Of course not," I soothed.

His fingers traced a path along the ceiling tiles. "Ugh, there's traces of him everywhere, which makes it harder to pinpoint him."

"But you'll find him?" I said.

"Sure, sure." He jumped down from the table. "What have you got there?"

Hells. "Nothing."

Devon grabbed my hands and pried my fingers apart. The pixie hopped off and onto a desk.

"Devon! Don't. Don't let the demon get his way." The pixie hopped over another desk. Another. Devon lunged, but I kicked his shins hard and that slowed him down. There was an open window, and I hoped the pixie had enough brains to go out it.

Devon darted up and around me, but his shoe hit a desk. I lunged for where he fell, but then he was no longer there. He appeared in a flash in front of the pixie, blocking the open window, moving with demonic speed.

The pixie levitated, blinking.

"Devon!" I shouted. "You don't need it, remember? To fill your contract the pixies just have to be here on Friday. It's Friday. You could let it go."

Devon's eyes narrowed. Then he lunged, I lunged, and then— the pixie was gone and the two of us were on a tangled heap on the floor. I looked down at Devon's clutched fists, swallowing. I couldn't even think about how interesting it was to be lying in a tangled heap with Devon—I was too focused on what might be in his hands.

But when he opened them, there was nothing.

The pixie had escaped.

Devon's face was suffused with rage as he jumped up. "I almost had it."

I seized his shoulders and shook hard. "Devon! I know you're still in there. Believe me, you can come out. Or shove him in, whatever metaphor you need."

This time took the longest. There was a full minute of me holding Devon's arms while he stared past me. But he didn't make those trying-not-to-puke faces this time as he came back. He was merely silent, and then he blinked and said, "Cam?"

"Crap," I said. "You are not holding on very well." That probably wasn't the most encouraging thing to say.

"I don't understand this, Cam," Devon said. His green eyes were worried. "It's not like a tug-of-war anymore. Not like I have to shove him aside. It's like . . . he's inside my brain."

"Well . . . he is."

Devon shook his head and that black hair flopped over one eyebrow. "No, it's weirder than that. It's like . . ." He swallowed. "It's like he's been inside me all along. Like a part of me that's always been waiting to come out. It's like we're one person."

"Wow." Every time I thought I understood the trickiness of demons, Estahoth came up with new ways to influence his host. "So he's messing with your mind like some kind of pulpy super-villain? Makes you want to destroy sophomore girls' lives for no reason?" Reese's distraught face was still very much in my mind.

Devon shook his head. "If it were for no reason, it'd be obvious." He moved closer and suddenly I was super-uncomfortable, like I was standing in a furnace. His eyes . . . were they earnest or menacing? The green was lost in shadow. "It's more that certain things seem like a good idea nowadays."

I tugged on my T-shirt. "Certain things like looking for a phoenix here at school? It's going to explode, you know."

"Certain things like taking a little time out from saving the world," he said. He put one hand on the radiator behind me and then he was leaning in. "The demon doesn't own me, you know. The witch doesn't own you."

"Well, no . . . but we have to stop her, you see . . . Time is running out . . ."

He was very close and that electricity was jumping around between us again. This *was* Devon, wasn't it? Devon on a very slippery slope?

He was very, very close. Low and velvety he sang, "She stands next to me, when the bad guys come around . . ."

I was not going to melt. I was not going to melt.

"I can control him," Devon said. "We can do this without him eating your dreams."

I was dying to believe him. But if I became Zombie Cam, everything was going to go to hell in a handbasket. I was *not* going to be Reese, and I was going to tell him that firmly, too. Barely I managed: "Not yet."

"When?"

"When this is over. If you still want to. If it's not just the demon speaking."

"It's not," he said. His lips brushed my cheek and I closed my eyes, blood rushing hot and loud through my skull. That's when I lost all my common sense. If he had decided to follow up the cheek with the lips, I would've been a total goner. I know, I know. I have no shame. I'm just telling you how it went down, and as often as not, how it went down is embarrassing.

I was at his mercy and he didn't kiss me.

I don't know if that was good or bad.

When I finally opened my eyes he was standing across the room, at the classroom door.

I hadn't heard him move.

"That's another chance you missed," he said softly. He tossed a dry-erase marker at me and then he was gone. The marker slipped through my fingers and clattered to the floor. I looked down at my feet.

On the floor where he had stood was a loosely sketched red pentagram. As I watched, a breeze slipped through the open window and, impossibly, blew it into fine red dust.

"His powers are developing *and* he knows I'm trying to trap him in a pentagram. We're screwed. How am I going to trick him inside of one now?" Jenah and I cut Sixth Hour and holed up in the second-floor rest room with my backpack of swiped books. I dosed the tiled floor liberally with unicorn sanitizer before we sat.

"Give me another of those books and I'll keep looking," said

Jenah. "Think outside the box. What's like a pentagram that's not a pentagram?"

"If math were my strong suit, I'd have goat's blood ready to go," I said. I leaned back against a bathroom stall. The tile was cold on my back and butt and I could smell the janitor's antiseptic mixed with my own, more powerful one. I shuffled the Tupperwares of spell ingredients around in my backpack until I found the book about demons. I set the heavy book on my knees.

"Mustard flickered in your aura right now," said Jenah, "so I don't really want you to explain that cryptic statement. We'll leave our galactic jump rope tangled this time."

"He's really very nice," I said. "Maybe *you'd* like to go to the dance with him tonight."

"Say no more. I see how it all went down between you and Mustard Man," said Jenah. She cradled a tall skinny book between her crossed legs. She had on an orange cotton skirt and red tights, and the tights went pink where they stretched over her knees. "Anyone could've seen it coming a mile away."

"Well, I didn't," I said glumly. I flicked over several pages and wondered why I never got around to wearing skirts. "So I'm almost ready with the demon-loosening spell, but unless we can find a substitution for goat's blood, we're screwed. What'd you find in there?"

"Substitutions for goat's blood," said Jenah.

"Brilliant," I said. "Read it off."

"'Cow's blood, though your spell will be weaker,'" read Jenah. "'Antelope blood, though your spell will be meeker. Donkey blood, though your spell will be bleaker.' Bleaker? How can a spell be bleak?"

"Some witch was too fond of being clever, if you ask me," I said. I shifted my butt on the cold tile. "We're not going to find any of those any more quickly than the goat's blood. Well, we could buy a package of hamburger, but trust me, we don't want the spell to be weaker."

"Do you know anyone else with goats?"

"Yeah, I finally thought of one," I said. "The guy who raises unicorns also has goats. The thing is, he's seriously creepy, and I really don't want to call him except as a last resort." I looked at the clock on my cell phone. "Unfortunately, the time is last-resort o'clock."

"Unicorns?" said Jenah. "Unicorns are real? Are they elementals, too?"

"Nope, just the three I told you about. 'Dragon, phoenix, and demon fell . . .' Unicorns do have a lot of magic in them, though. They get used for spells, like that vodka purifier I cleaned you with. Once a witch puts the ingredients together, anyone can use that spell because it stands alone pretty well. Vodka, one drop of dragon milk, one unicorn hair."

"I guess I'm fuzzy on the difference."

"Unicorns may be all purifying and stuff, but they're just animals," I said. "They're mortal. Unlike elementals, they can be changed by witch magic—that's the main spell performed on them, in fact, to hide their horns so they can pass. If they weren't full of useful sheddy bits I don't know who'd bother to keep them. They're not very intelligent and they're mean as all get-out."

"You've seen one?" said Jenah. "Out at Creepy Guy's place?"

"Seen one just last month, disguised as a llama," I said. "Nearly took my arm off."

"Wouldn't it be smarter to disguise them as horses?"

"A common mistake," I said. I hadn't told anyone witch stuff since Sparkle, when I was five. I'd forgotten how much fun it was to be the expert on a subject others found fascinating. To be able to shatter the myths they thought they knew. "Unicorns actually look a lot like llamas."

"Unicorn llamas," said Jenah, eyebrows up. "Fuzzy? Woolly? Soft?"

"Yup," I said. My ingrained caution tried to stop me from saying the next part, but as long as I was going to trust Jenah, then I ought to show her some of the fun parts of being tied to the witch as well. "I'll show you someday."

"It might be worth a trip to Creepy Guy's place."

I shuddered. "No. But I'm sure he's not the only guy with unicorns. I'll keep an ear out." I turned more pages of the demon book. "Okay, pentagrams can be made of anything," I read. "As long as the circuit is complete. Many things have been used to attempt to trick demons into being caught in pentagrams, since nobody likes a demon on the loose. One unusual pentagram that caught the demon Bezerath was made of an unbroken stream of water. The pentagram was a shallow trough in the ground. The witch ran a garden hose into it while activating the pentagram. The demon was caught, along with a confused squirrel."

Jenah shut her book with a thump. "So the question is, what do we possibly have that we can get near to him, that won't alert him? Not to dim those nice sparkly blue bits that just appeared in your aura, but if we surround him with five brooms or try to quick-fling five streamers around him, he'll notice real fast."

"Ah, but we do have something," I said. "In fact, we have five somethings."

14

Halloween Dance

If the awesomeness of a dance can be judged by the number of streamers, then the Halloween Dance Committee had outdone themselves. There were black and silver ones everywhere. Starry black balloons trailing twenty-foot silver ribbons bounced against the ceiling.

Most everyone entering the gym was in costume. Lots of boys with dripping blood faces and lots of girls in miniskirt cat costumes. Witches, too. But all the witches were cute and wore stripey tights and tiny pointy hats.

None of them looked like the evil witches I knew.

Including the one stalking right through the gym doors with me in a pencil skirt and support hose. "I expect this will be quite dull," Sarmine said. "Luckily we shall be spending most of the evening elsewhere."

"Good," I said. "Why don't you start now?"

"Nonsense. I must check in with your choir teacher. I don't want to be an unsupervised adult on the school premises."

"Fine time to worry about that," I said. "Why don't you tell them what you're up to while you're at it?"

"Oh, there's that interesting root beer–smelling man," she said. "Did you doppelgänger yourself like I suggested?"

"I made up the test and improved my grade like you didn't suggest," I said. "Still didn't stop you from coming to school. Are you planning to do anything embarrassing tonight?"

"I think I'll go say hi to him," the witch said. "It's rather nice to talk to a man who doesn't want to cheat me on the price of unicorn hairs. It's been a long time since Jim."

"Jim Hexar?" I said. "Of Hexar/Scarabouche?"

She studied me as if I were a pinned insect. "Who else?"

"Witchipedia said he disappeared in a demon mishap."

"Jim was too nice, just like I caution you about. It got in his way again and again. I remember one time he refused to work the fortune-telling spell, simply because it used live mice. When of course, that's what mice are *for*. I spent a long time being angry with him for disappearing on us."

"On *us*?" I said.

I swear, the witch rolled her eyes at that point. But I couldn't question her further because Jenah showed up. Jenah stuck out her hand to be introduced and kept her face as bland as if she had no idea that this was the woman who had rolled me up in a pumpkin patch.

"It's a pleasure to meet you," said Jenah.

"I suppose it must be," said Sarmine.

Jenah shook her head. "You two look so much alike."

"Thank you," said the witch. "That's quite a compliment." She did not specify to whom.

"Ostensibly this woman is here as a school parent," I said. "It's the school's lucky day."

"Oh, there's your choir teacher," said Sarmine. "Talking to my root-beer man. Who does she think she is?" She stalked over in that direction.

I cringed, but there didn't seem to be anything I could do about any of that at this point. So I rounded on Jenah, who was saying, "You don't take choir."

"We are *not* related," I said. "Why do you say those things?"

"Are you sure?" she said. "*A*, your auras are like totally different colors—but they have the exact same spiky green brightnesses around the head. I think it's a witch thing. *B*, you make the same face when you're about to get stubborn. She looks like she could be your older sister. You didn't tell me she was so young."

"Witches look like whatever age they feel on the inside," I said. "She usually looks sixty." I peered through the dim dance lights to where Sarmine was apparently speaking politely to both Miss Crane and Visible Undershirt. "She does look awfully young tonight. Maybe that's what fooled you into thinking you saw similarities."

Jenah wrinkled her nose.

"Now look. I have an idea about what to do with the phoe-nix power," I said. "So it doesn't explode and cause fire and destruction and hells knows what else. But I can't do it without you."

"Okay," said Jenah dubiously. "I can't control an elemental, if that's what you mean. I just see auras."

I shook my head. "The demon will do that part of it," I said. "But look." I breathed deep and handed her the keys to Moon-fire's garage. "Can you get the dragon up here?"

Jenah looked down at the keys, and I think in that moment she saw how much I did trust her. I mean, not just letting her into my life, but I was giving her the keys to something that represented all the ways I was different from everybody else. How metaphorical was that? It was the sort of thing you wrote five-paragraph English essays on.

Jenah took the keys from me. "I will."

"I'm not ruining your evening by asking, am I?"

"God, no," said Jenah. "Real witches instead of an-excuse-to-wear-a-miniskirt witches? I'm all in." Jenah herself was in a black-and-white-striped miniskirt, tights, and shirt, with a painted-on broken neck ("I'm a crosswalk," she explained later), but as she always dressed in miniskirts, she was allowed.

"Good," I said. I checked my phone: 8:05. "You have thirty-five minutes." That was assuming we found the phoenix, of course. "Um, if you see the school explode, don't come back."

I checked my phone yet again and saw the message light blinking. Creepy unicorn guy had returned my Phone Call of Last Resort. I nerved myself and listened to his message. It said he would love to supply me with goat's blood, and in exchange all he would ask was for me to pose with one of his unicorns for the calendar he was working on. In something schoolgirly, like those cute Japanese girls wear. He started describing the potential outfit in more detail, but I hit "delete" as fast as possible.

So that was now my only option for goat's blood, and if I had to trade something besides cash for blood, obviously I would've picked dance-with-Kelvin in a heartbeat, not that I had that option anymore. I wasn't in love with Kelvin, but Kelvin was not creepy. If I *had* crushed on Kelvin, maybe that would've made everything go more smoothly.

But *could* I crush on Kelvin? I didn't think so.

I pondered what Kelvin would be like as a boyfriend, rather than dialing that phone number, as I knew I was going to have to do. But I was just putting off the inevitable.

I picked up my phone.

And then a tall guy with a wide pale face strode stiffly into the room. He was wrapped in aluminum foil from head to toe, with occasional green ruffles.

Kelvin.

I was sure he wouldn't want to talk to me any more than I wanted to talk to him right now, so I turned toward the stage where Blue Crush (minus Devon) was setting up. I looked down at my call log to find Creepy Guy's number. Maybe Kelvin and I could pretend we hadn't seen each other.

But a crinkling sound proclaimed that he now stood next to me.

"Um. Hi," I said. "What are you?"

"Leftovers," Kelvin said. "Specifically, a leftover six-foot sub. Feast your eyes on the lettuce sticking out. I made the lettuce out of an old dust ruffle. I made the foil out of foil."

"Clever," I said. "I'm afraid I'm just me. Maybe I could be leftover me. The me after I've had a very long week."

There was silence except for the crinkling of his aluminum. The dance lights twinkled off his foil. His lettuce ruffles danced in the breeze from the heating vent.

Then Kelvin said: "I lied before. You know what about."

"About the pig flu. About liking me. About how to multiply exponents. About the fertilization of chicken eggs. About the earth being flat. About the *goat's blood*?"

"It was cow's blood," he said. "The goats were being grouchy and my mother didn't think it would matter. I didn't want to be the one who messed up your experiment, so . . . I used my acting skills on you to pretend I hadn't. It's a violation of theater ethics *and* 4-H ethics. I'm sorry. I know deep down you already knew all this and that's why you despised me."

"Kelvin. I do *not* despise you. I just like someone else and I can't help that." I put on my best robot voice: "Love is strange and nonmechanical. Does not compute."

For once, Kelvin smiled.

Then he held out a cooler. "No payment due," he said.

Relief, brilliant bold relief. Kissing Kelvin's cheek would be a bad idea, but I hugged his arm. "Thank goodness," I said. "Ooh, I crinkled your foil."

He looked down at me. "It's more authentic now," he said.

"Right," I said. Awkwardly. "Look, I'll see you later, okay? I've got an experiment to get going."

He nodded and lurched off to talk to a boy in a sparkly dragon T-shirt, not saying good-bye.

I looked at the items on my latest list and made a couple
more notes.

- Trap Devon in a pentagram (blow on it and tap with
  wand to set the spell)
- Compound demon-loosening spell (in progress!)
- ~~Check and see if Devon has located the phoenix~~ JUST
  HOPE HE DOES

All I had to do was find Devon. And hope the zombie girls
were by the T-Bird, where Jenah told them to meet. I jumped
onstage even though Miss Crane turned from her convo with
Rourke and the witch to scold me from a distance. "Camellia,
dear, really, should you—"

"Hey guys," I said. "Have you seen Devon?"

The bassist shook his red dreads. "Not my day to watch him."

The guitar guy said, "No, and if he thinks he can get out of
setup just because he's singing lead instead of me . . !" He waved
the cords he was untangling.

"All righty then," I said, and stepped over black cords to go.

But the drummer said, "I saw him." The drummer turned
out to be a fine-boned black girl with piercings. She stopped
fiddling with her snare to point toward the side entrance. "He
finally got a reputation, huh? I kept telling him one day he'd
be dripping in girls."

I was suddenly jealous of this unknown girl for sharing Devon's life before I knew him. For bolstering him in his shyness.
For having a history. For being easy in her skin, like Jenah. For
being cooler than I was.

What I said was: "Thanks." I know she watched me go,
watched me jump off the stage and dart through the dance,
and I wondered if she thought I was hurrying to drip off him,
too.

Devon was by the T-Bird talking to some girl dressed as a miniskirted pirate. Miracle of miracles, four of the zombie girls were clustered nearby. This wasn't entirely due to the magnetic pull of Devon—I had tasked Jenah with phoning them all after school. She told them Devon had a little game for them, and to meet by the T-Bird.

Occasionally one wandered up to Devon and drove off the latest girl to stop and talk to him. Two zombie girls were dressed as witches and two as groupies, both of which seemed ironic. Reese had reverted to idiotic bliss, now that Devon was nearby and smiling her way.

I nodded to Reese and then dropped to the ground behind the mock orange with my backpack and Kelvin's cooler. I took out the apple-oyster glop for the demon-loosening spell, and carefully swirled in the last, precious ingredient.

"Over here, Avery," I heard Reese holler, and then the fifth zombie girl (a groupie) hurried from her mom's car up the hill to the T-Bird.

Reese drove off the pirate girl with a white-toothed snarl, and the zombie girls moved in around Devon.

"Hey chickies," said Devon. The actual suaveness the demon had learned from Devon receded as the demon got more and more confident that he had his claws in Devon for good, and the faux suaveness that the demon thought was totally the bomb had taken over. He had his collar flipped up again. "What do you girls want?"

"Kiss me," said the zombie girls in a ragged chorus.

"One kiss per satisfied customer," said Devon, shaking his finger. "Don't crowd me, sweet things." The girls sighed and obeyed, but they stayed in a loose circle around Devon.

Well, not quite a loose circle.

Only an observant observer would've noticed that the five

girls had evenly spaced themselves around the grinning boy in the middle. They smiled sweetly at Devon.

"This is the life," the demon said. He looked at the twilight sky as if he wanted to remember it forever. "This is the life."

That's when I said, "Now!"

The girls grabbed each other's hands with straight arms. I ran from the bushes, shoved the bowl of ingredients just between Reese's feet. I blew on her arm just as I brought my wand down upon her shoulder, freezing the pentagram in place. The magic jolted me just as it had when I tried the self-defense spell.

But this time I was ready for it. I held the wand on Reese's shoulder while beams of light shot up from all the girls.

Devon was enclosed in a living pentagram.

He expanded for a moment and rippled all colors, just like I'd first seen the demon. Rage was written all over him. Then he shrunk down into a black-haired punk-band boy. "Very funny," he said to me. "But a human pentagram has certain limitations. Reese, let me out of here." He motioned for her to drop the hand of the girl next to her.

"No thanks," Reese said sweetly.

"Ha. Come on."

"Nope," she said.

"Avery? Tashelle?"

The other girls shook their heads.

Devon glared at me. "What is this?"

"Cam said you said it's the only way to prove our love," said Reese in a singsong recitation. "Whoever holds on the longest wins you forever."

"For the evening," I corrected.

Devon turned a smoldering gaze on Reese. "Why don't you drop hands and I'll choose you right now?"

Reese looked dubious, but the girls on either side scowled

and held her tighter. She tugged a bit and gave up. "Nope," she said finally. "She said you'd test us to see who's weak. But my love is strong." Her eyes burned with zombie fire. "My love is eternal."

Devon reached out to force Reese and Avery's hands apart, but his hands stopped an invisible quarter inch from them. He tried to lean on the girls' hands, tried to push on them, tried to focus power onto them, but nothing. It looked like he couldn't touch the pentagram girl formation at all. Which is what the book had implied, but it was very reassuring to see it actually work.

"Why you . . ." he growled at me.

"Temper, temper," I said.

He smoothed his face. "It doesn't matter what you hope to do. I'm almost permanently embodied. Devon enjoys having me around, and once he feels the power of us controlling the phoenix, he'll never want me to go. We'll be together for all time."

I hoped the demon wasn't as confident as he seemed. "But you don't have his soul yet," I said. "And what you haven't noticed is that I stuck a loosening spell inside the pentagram with you. Devon, now's your chance. The demon's not bound to you anymore. You can push him out of you."

I held my breath and watched Devon freeze in the middle of the pentagram.

Tension. Waiting. Surely struggle must be passing behind his eyes, back where I couldn't see.

Finally he blinked and sneered. "Nearly have him for good," he repeated. "So what's the point of this charade?"

My shoulders sagged.

But it isn't over till it's over. "At the very least this keeps you where I can keep an eye on you," I told him. "Have you found the bird? Are you ready to transfigure it so the explosion can be controlled safely?"

"Found it ages ago," said Devon. "It was obvious."

"Good. Where is it?"

He snorted. "Let me out."

"Not till you're out of Devon," I said.

"Then it will explode," he said.

I narrowed my eyes. "Then the blast will take you down, too." I didn't plan to let it come to that. "Girls, don't let Devon down," I said. "Prove your love for him. Your own personal 'Hands on a Hard Body' competition."

"Ooohh," the girls sighed. Hands trembled.

"Except you can't let go!" I said hastily. "That part comes after."

"Awwww."

A few kids had stopped to take in the scene. They looked interested until I said, "It's a skit we're performing later in the evening."

"Lame," said one, and they hurried into the dance.

I checked my cell. Eighteen minutes to explosion. I'd better tear the witch away from Rourke.

The witch had already come to the same conclusion and was stalking out of the gym just as I was returning to find her. Someone's "spooky" playlist was blaring over the sound system, and I could see Blue Crush trying to tune beneath it.

"I captured the demon," I said breathlessly. "He knows where the phoenix is hidden and he's trying to keep the explosion for himself. So he's in a pentagram till we get down there."

"You tricked the demon into a pentagram?" A strange emotion crossed the witch's face. It couldn't possibly be pride, so it must be anger or jealousy. And then: "You did a spell?"

"Yup," I said. "Two, if you count the pentagram. Proving that anyone can do magic if you gather the right ingredients."

The witch shook her head. "Ingredients are only half. It takes your internal magic to push the rest."

"Right, but all organisms have magic," I said. "Therefore all humans have magic, witch blood or no. So why not? What's the difference?"

"The difference between a frog and a pixie," said the witch. "The difference between a llama and a unicorn. A very big difference."

"Bosh," I said. "Then how come I could work the spells?"

The witch looked me straight in the eye. "Obviously, Camellia," she said, "because you're my daughter."

15

CASH

This is how I felt.

I felt like the world had stopped around me and broke into two sections—before, when I thought I was a regular human, and now.

Because deep down I knew the witch—my mother—was telling the truth.

Age lines creased Sarmine's face, bringing her up to forty-ish. "Some friend of yours told you it was bad to be a witch. Remember?"

I cringed. "Sparkle. Yes."

"The two of you concocted a new story about how I stole you from your parents in some heinous Rapunzel-like scheme. As if any witch would want an ordinary human child." Her face abruptly aged to that of familiar sixtyish Sarmine. "But that's what I got."

It seemed like a moment to say I was sorry, but I couldn't feel it. Conflicting emotions shuddered through me—disappointment, stress, guilt. And underneath, a small sliver of . . . excitement? "I . . . I didn't know," I said lamely.

"I know," said the witch. "That six-year-old girl was like some kind of Svengali. You were obsessed with trying to be what she wanted. And when she didn't want you to be a witch, you convinced yourself you weren't. I tried to make you admit the truth so many times. Eventually I just gave up."

I thought back to when I was five and any urge to say "I'm

sorry" vanished. "You're wrong," I said. "It wasn't her, it was you. We *saw* you. We saw you in the basement, working a spell. A really horrible spell. *That's* why I didn't want to be a witch."

It was the witch's turn to be surprised. "What spell?"

I swallowed. "I've seen you use a bunch of ingredients I think are awful," I said. "But I've never seen you actually kill something yourself. Except that day."

The witch went white. "You saw the tracing spell," she said. "I never knew."

"That's why I didn't want to be a witch," I said. "I *couldn't* be." I had never seen Sarmine at a loss for words and I didn't know what to make of it. "We'd better get back to the demon," I said awkwardly, and turned, but Sarmine touched my arm.

"It was my last chance to find Jim," she said, her lips ghastly pale. "And it failed."

"Jim Hexar."

She nodded.

"Camellia Anna Stella Hendrix," I said. "But my real name isn't Hendrix, is it? It's Hexar. It always was."

"The neighbors had a dog named Hendrix," she said. She shook her head, her color returning. "I never knew you saw. When you came home with your new name and story, I aged twenty years in a day. It was like between the two of you, you put some sort of block on yourself. Witches are secretive and paranoid and hide things from each other, but you two took it to extremes."

"Sparkle's that kind of girl already, though," I said. "She hides everything. Like she hates that she doesn't have parents. She lives with her grandfather on the Japanese side, and she won't admit that she's an orphan and they're broke and everything else. Like if she doesn't mention whatever it was that happened to her parents, she can block it out, re-create her life."

"Her Japanese grandfather—" said the witch, suddenly staring at me. "Camellia, I always thought you were the one who managed the block. But what if—" She controlled her rising voice. "What if your friend was from a witch family, too? Kari—Hikari—was also Japanese."

"Kari?" The name was familiar.

"The witch who hid R-AB1 fourteen years ago right here in this school. Really, Camellia, don't you ever listen?"

Shock ran through me as I pieced this together. "Did Kari have a daughter?" I said.

The witch frowned. "I don't think so. But perhaps Sparkle is a niece or cousin." She looked bemused. "If her grandfather is the witch-blood side, then he's sure been lying low."

I shook my head, bewildered but certain. "Sparkle is a witch, too," I said. "I'm almost sure of it. That's the missing piece, the only thing that makes sense." I ran through the clues again but came up with the same answer. And . . . "Oh hells, I left the demon locked in a pentagram. If there's a witch on the loose—or a whole family of them—we'd better make sure he's still in that pentagram."

The witch was bone-still, thinking. "It doesn't quite fit," she said. "You girls were five and six years old. Even if she saw my spell, why would she care whether or not you thought you were a witch?"

"Duh, because she was embarrassed about being one herself," I said.

The witch's eyebrows drew together and for the first time, I saw her honestly puzzled. "Why would she be embarrassed about that?"

I shook my head. "Sarmine Scarabouche, you do not remember what it was like to be five, or even fifteen," I said. "Now help me find Sparkle before she throws a monkey wrench in the works."

I ran out of the gym and down the hall, the witch clip-clopping behind me in her heels. "Where are the hundred pixies?" she said.

"Last I saw they were being squished on the rooftop," I said. It didn't hurt to tell her, because she wasn't going to get to use that spell. Especially not now that there was one pixie missing.

"I'll send Estahoth after them after we release him from the pentagram," said Sarmine. "What about my hopes and dreams? Did he get those?"

"The proof is in the pentagram," I said.

We skidded out the side door. The living pentagram still stood.

Standing next to the T-Bird was Sparkle.

Not surprisingly, she was dressed as a princess, in a rose gown covered in various shades of pinky-rose sequins from shoulders to train. A tiara perched on her glossy straight hair.

The witch rapped the glassy air between two of the girls. "Nice work," she said. "A little watery-sounding. Your breath must have betrayed nerves. Still, not bad for your first try."

There was, I admit, a small glow created by the words "Nice work," coming from the witch. I suppressed it.

"What are you doing here?" I said to Sparkle as the witch poked the air.

"I—I don't know," said Sparkle. She was doing the now-familiar gesture of clutching her cameo.

"Oh, right," I said sarcastically. "No clever plan at all. Nothing that involves being . . . a witch."

Sparkle wet her lips. "No!" she said. "Nothing like that. I just—I just got this feeling, okay? Like there was something I was supposed to do over here by the T-Bird."

The T-Bird.

Of course.

"The phoenix," Sarmine said reverently. She left the pentagram and crossed to the statue, her heels squishing points in the dirt. Devon and the zombie girls watched as Sarmine raised her hands reverently to the bird's head. She closed her eyes, running her fingers over the head of the transfigured elemental. Silence filled the air.

"It's not it," said Sarmine.

"What?" I saw shock on Devon's face, too. The T-Bird made so much sense.

"I can't be positive, but . . . it doesn't have that elemental feeling. It feels like plain metal." Sarmine looked at Devon, bound in the pentagram. "Well, there's one way to find out. Time to get the demon out of there. He knows."

"No!" I said sharply.

"No?"

I pointed to the bowl inside the pentagram. "He's not tied into Devon right now. You want him loose?"

The witch's face went rigid. "A loosening spell? Why would you do that? What kind of idiot—?" She composed her face. "We have to let him out regardless. He has to transfigure the phoenix and harness its power before it explodes. The power can only be contained safely if the phoenix is in its proper form."

Devon shook his head wildly. There was fear on his face as the demon realized he had failed one of his tasks. "I don't know where it is."

"That's your third task," Sarmine said. "You must."

"I was so sure it was the phoenix. I know it's near. I can feel its presence here in the school. It's lonely and cold and hard."

"It's *got* to be the T-Bird," I said. "What else would it be?"

"I don't know," said Sarmine. "What else would it be, *Hikari*?"

Sparkle backed away from us. "How do you know my real name? Are you a teacher?"

"I didn't recognize you when you were six," said Sarmine. "But you can't hide anymore. Tell us where the phoenix is. You're the one who summoned a demon to hide it. You're the one who knows."

"I don't know what you're talking about!"

Sarmine whipped out her dragon-milk wand, scattered a white powder in front of it, and flicked it at Sparkle, slamming the girl backward. "Tell us," she said.

"What are you doing?" I rushed toward the witch, but she forestalled me with a flick of the wand.

"You stopped me before. You won't stop me this time, Hikari," said Sarmine.

"Stop calling me Hikari!" shouted Sparkle. She clutched her cameo necklace as she fought off Sarmine's force.

"What do you have in that charm? Dragon scales glued to the back? You were always a scaly sort of hag."

Sparkle was staying upright only by a huge effort. We all saw her nose suddenly flick back to its crooked form.

"Ha!" cried Sarmine. "It's keeping your nose job on, isn't it? How'd you figure out that spell?"

"Envelope to me . . . said not to open till I was fifteen . . . then I could have the nose I always wanted . . ." Sparkle's eyes darted, and the words were an effort. "Followed the weird algebra problem with rhubarb and horsehairs and then suddenly this happened." She gestured at her straight nose.

"So her mom left her a spell?" I said.

"Not her mom," said Sarmine. "Considering the source it was vaguely clever. All Kari had to do was an amnesia spell on herself. Ten years ago after she transfigured the phoenix and had to hide until its rebirth, she made herself forget almost everything. Made herself think she was six. And then—"

"Because witches look on the outside like the age they feel inside . . ." I said.

Sarmine nodded. "For all practical purposes she *was* six."

Sparkle was pale. "It's not true," she said.

"Probably dropped herself off at her grandfather's with a note from 'Mom,'" said Sarmine. "'Take care of my daughter' et cetera. Is that right? You live with your grandfather?"

"I do . . ." Sparkle shook her head wildly and I admit I felt kinda bad for her. "It's not true! I'm not *old*. I'm not!"

"Oh yes, you are," Sarmine said grimly. "And I bet you have another note that you were supposed to follow today, to summon a demon to control the phoenix. Did you balk at that spell?"

Sparkle looked at me, and I think in that moment we both remembered tiptoeing halfway down the basement stairs, curious. Holding on to the cold railing and each other. Watching pretty red smoke curls, watching silver stars. Then watching Sarmine sacrifice a ferret in a pool of crimson blood.

"The spell called for goat's blood," Sparkle whispered.

Sarmine looked at her bracelet watch. "Six minutes till the explosion." To me: "Get your wand out."

"How did you know I've got—" She glared and I shut up. "Right."

"You never were a very clever witch, were you, Hikari?" Sarmine was needling Sparkle, throwing her off balance. In a low voice she said: "To find the phoenix, I have to lift the spell so she remembers everything."

I could tell from Sarmine's posture that she was braced. Hikari might not be the best witch in the world—and she probably didn't have a store of ingredients close to hand like Sarmine did—but she was about to have all her power and memory back, and she wasn't going to like us very much. I gripped my wand.

Sarmine's free hand was rummaging through her fanny pack. "A sprig of parsley," she muttered. "Three alder leaves . . . we'll substitute elm. Four faux gems . . ." She ripped off the two pearl buttons on the high neck of her shirt. "Cam, six elm leaves and two more things like gemstones. Now."

Of course you know where the gemstone-like things were. In what I supposed was irony, I tackled Sparkle, who was busy watching the witch root through the fanny pack. "I'm sorry," I gasped out. "But otherwise the phoenix . . . will incinerate . . . us all." I grappled for her tiara, but she wouldn't let it go.

"You're as bad as she is," hissed Sparkle, which made me lose the sympathy for her I'd just had. Honestly, she was as aggravating as Sarmine Scarabouche. Why couldn't people be all good or all bad? This business with feeling sorry for someone who could turn around and be obnoxious the next minute made things so complicated.

The witch pulled off her shoe and pulverized her ingredients in it. "Counterfeit money would work, too," she said. "Something that imitates something valuable."

"Oh, that's you, all right," I said to Sparkle. She bit my arm.

"Humans invest belief in fakes," the witch lectured. "We agree to regard Hikari's tiara as imitating something expensive. And the expensive item itself is something that's only expensive because we believe in its value. A gemstone rarely has intrinsic worth, except for diamonds, which are used to cut things, and opals, which will keep all insects from biting you."

Sparkle shoved me off and I fell, cradling my arm. One last ploy to prevent that phoenix explosion. "I've got my phone in my pocket," I told Sparkle. "You want your picture back? So you can go back to pretending your nose didn't straighten out magically?" I held it out, and when she brought the tiara up indecisively, I grabbed it and dropped the phone into her hands.

I tossed the tiara at Sarmine, who caught it. With her wand she poked two jewels from it and they fell in her shoe.

"Press seven-oh-four to unlock it. Then scroll and delete," I told Sparkle.

Sparkle's fingers flew. I don't think she even cared as Sarmine threw the contents of her shoe at Sparkle and traced the air with her wand in a star pattern.

The air whirled around Sparkle. For a moment, she lost all color, like she was a sepia photograph. "Whoa," said one of the zombie girls. Then Sparkle colorized, in pieces, and as she did her head jerked up as if she was remembering things, great gallons of things, all at once. The phone dropped to the ground and blinked off, dead.

"Not again," I said.

And while Sparkle was distracted, Sarmine shouted, "The phoenix is exploding!"

Which made Sparkle jump backward.

And look directly at the ground in front of the T-Bird.

Sparkle's head shot up again and she sneered, but it was too late.

"The mouse," I said. "It's the mouse statue! That's almost clever."

"What would you know, Cash," said Sparkle.

She was growing taller now, filling out. She was a college chick, she was an adult, she was older and older. Her waist thickened, then silver threaded her hair, then tiny creases sprouted under her eyes and on the backs of her hands.

Until at last she looked the same age as Sarmine.

Sparkle stared in disbelief at her hands. "No," she whispered. "No, this is not me."

"Did you really try to convince me I was normal?" I said.

"We *are* normal," she said, voice screeching upward. "I don't want to be Kari. I don't want these memories. I don't want to be evil."

The witch snorted. "You always were an idiot." She turned

to me. "Ready to release the demon? I need to finish making my spell so we can capture the explosion and use it to get enough power to run the town. I need those pixies, for starters."

"Tough," I said, and surprise pinched her features. "One of the pixies got away. You've only got ninety-nine left."

Her face cleared. "That's all right. I only need fifty."

"You had the demon kill an extra fifty pixies just to make sure you had enough?"

"I wasn't leaving anything to chance. Now release the demon, please. Unless you want the phoenix to explode." She pulled a collapsible bowl from her fanny pack, snapped it into shape, and set it on the ground. She measured off various contents of her pack into it.

"You want me to help you," I said. "I've been working all week to stop you. You know what? I'm getting off this merry-go-round."

The witch tapped a teaspoon of something blue into the bowl. "So you're ready to be reasonable?"

"I can't win if I play your game," I said. "You've got me backed into a corner where all I can do is help you take over the city, or stop you from that but let a school full of innocent people die. I choose the third way. I choose to use the phoenix power myself."

The witch stirred the powders in her bowl with a metal baby spoon. "You don't have the ingredients for that," she said calmly. "I know you don't have the spell—I researched for fifteen years to find out how to harness something so close to elemental power, even with the demon's help. And you certainly don't have the power, you and that Goody Two-shoes little wand and your day's worth of spell practice. You can't do it."

"I can if I use an elemental."

16

Demon Girl

I'd never seen Sarmine look scared before. "I just reclaimed my daughter," she said grimly. "I don't want an embodied demon instead." She stood, clutching her bowl.

"You won't get one," I said with more confidence than I felt. I knocked on the pentagram between Reese and Avery. It was solid. But the pentagram spell had hinted that the witch who made the pentagram had certain powers over it. *You are mine*, I told it. *I made you. Let me in.* The pentagram went kind of spongy around my hand.

"Sure, it'll let you in. But it won't let you out," warned Sarmine. "I know pentagrams."

"Human pentagrams have certain limitations," I told her.

She moved toward me, but I ducked under Reese's and Avery's arms and wiggled inside.

"Hey! How come you—" squealed Reese, but the other girls kept a grip on her hands. I breathed a silent hope that they'd hold her down.

It was very weird being inside a pentagram. Everything on the outside was transmuted through the rainbowy glass. The girls' faces seemed all wavery, and when they spoke, they sounded underwater. Out of curiosity, I tried to touch Reese's shoulder, but my finger stopped that quarter inch from her witch costume.

The witch walked around the pentagram, tapping for

entrance. But she had already said, "Good work," so I tried not to worry.

"What exactly do you hope to accomplish?" Arms crossed, Devon sneered at me.

His eyes were so cold when he was the demon. I stared into them, remembering them warm and kind and full of light.

He shifted under my gaze.

"Think of your dog," I said, "the one who likes those pig's ears, think of him running to you. Think of the old animal shelter. Think of a day when you tried to walk six dogs at once and wrapped yourself around a tree."

"Oh, that will tempt him," said Estahoth.

"Think of the song you wrote about it later. Think of sitting on the school lawn with your guitar, working on your songs. You remember finding the pixies? Think of doing that again, but without him. Walking slowly along the creek, watching the pixies blink on and off. Watching bats swoop after mosquitoes. Writing a song about these things," I said. "These are all the things *you* like. Estahoth doesn't care about any of this. You let him stay and you'll belong to him forever. How long will Estahoth play by your rules if he doesn't have to? Will he let you keep your band? Your songwriting?" I held his eyes. "Your friends?"

Devon bent double, breaking eye contact. I soldiered on.

"Think of what he did to the pixies," I said. "Of course you didn't want to talk about that before. He didn't want you to. Maybe he misjudged how much it would take to break you. We're talking about it now. Think of ninety-nine tiny green pixies, with glowing wings. Think of squishing them to goo, think of how the bones cracked between your fingers. Think of being like someone who does everything you hate. Remember when you said that to me in the hallway?"

I touched his shoulder. He was shaking. "Think of choosing your own path. You can be you again, all you. Just tell him to go."

Silence.

And then rainbow light came streaming from his skin. The light was force and power and it beat me back, into the side of the pentagram, which didn't budge. The firecracker/mold smell was strong and pungent here in the confines of the pentagram, and I sneezed but didn't flinch. It was Tuesday afternoon all over again, except this time things were different.

This time I was letting the demon in.

Demons rush to bodies. I opened wide and let the elemental stream into me. He wailed when he realized where he was, and tried to leave.

"Oh no, you don't," I said. "You're staying right here." I kept him locked inside me, which—although an unbelievably creepy sensation, like keeping a live goldfish imprisoned in your mouth—wasn't impossible. After all, demons longed for human bodies. Estahoth wanted to leave me and try Devon again, but at the same time I was his raincoat, his shelter from the storm. The force of my command to him worked on him somewhat, as the witch's had on Tuesday. He cowered in me, ambivalent, huddling. "You're still not done with your contract," I told him. "But first we're releasing these hopes and dreams to their rightful owners."

The demon calmed down, coiled. The goldfish sensation lessened. I felt him lurking, felt a mental shrug. "Fine," said Estahoth. But if he was willing to play my game for the moment, then he must be thinking of some new plan. I didn't trust him an inch. "My part of the bargain was fulfilled by collecting them."

And then all five dreams that he'd collected bubbled up in me. I sorted through them. Reese's secret hope to be a kindergarten teacher and have a big family. Avery's fierce desire to be a tennis star. The girl who liked computers wanted to design games, Tashelle wanted to build bridges, and the last girl wanted to be a librarian. I sent all the dreams back to them, and the pentagram shimmered and cracked apart as one by one they dropped hands.

Well, except Reese, who still clung to the hands next to her, even when the girls tried to push her off. "I won, I won," she said, near tears. The glassy zombie stare was gone, but her face was crumpled and confused.

Devon wavered and fell to his knees in the mud. "I'm sorry, Reese," he said, and there was a crack in his voice. "All of you." Most of the girls wandered off looking dazed, but Avery slapped him upside the head as she pulled heartbroken Reese away.

"My hopes and dreams!" shrieked the witch. "How can I harness the phoenix now?"

"*You* harness the phoenix?" shouted Sparkle/Kari. Her face was distraught, but her memory must have been sorting itself into place. It seemed to be pulling her in two directions, almost like I'd seen with Devon/Estahoth. That was surely all her former Kari-self yelling, "That was *my* phoenix. I discovered it and brought it here. He's all mine!"

"Not if I get to him first," said Sarmine.

"You've got a dragon," shot back Kari. "What do you need a phoenix for, too? Greedy, evil—"

"Guys, guys," I said. "Nobody owns a phoenix. You can't own a phoenix any more than you can a human."

And I reached down deep to the coiled elemental who still had one more part of his contract to fulfill. "Ready?" I said.

"Ready," said Estahoth.

His force running through mine, we reached down and clasped the tiny metal mouse. There was a moment where we were working in harmony, and it felt right, like we understood each other and knew each other inside and out.

And I suddenly thought, Is this something that was part of Devon that I liked, that now will be gone forever?

But under our hands the mouse was warming. It came free from its base and we picked it up, warming, growing, changing in our hands. It was red, it was orange, it smelled of cinnamon and heartbeats, it fluttered, it breathed, it grew.

It lifted from my hands, still growing. Bigger, and bigger, until it was the size of Moonfire. Then bigger still, and I saw now that its feathers were dulled and torn with age, that its eyes were pouched, that its tail was heavy. The phoenix was very old. It was ready for rebirth. It was ready to start over.

"Thirty seconds," said the witch.

Behind the phoenix I saw a form beating toward us, approaching in invisible sweeps that blocked the stars. "Cam!" whooped a far-off voice. "Cam!"

"Come," said the demon. "See what we can do." And with Estahoth's help I seemed to grow out of my body, expanding along with the phoenix, which rose and winged higher and higher. "What is it you want to do with the flame? We can do anything. You could follow Sarmine's lead. Use it to control the city. Or use it to control Sarmine."

Unlimited power.

Anything I wanted.

"R-AB1," I whispered into the night. "Will you grant me the force of your fire?"

There was a strange moment as I found that the phoenix spoke not in images like the dragon, nor words like the demon, but in emotion. A pure giddy feeling swept over me that could only be agreement.

"Look what I can do for you," said Estahoth. "You couldn't do this without me."

"I know," I said. "Believe me, I know."

And then the phoenix burst into flame.

Estahoth reached out through me and like a current we transmuted the force of the explosion. Unlike Sarmine, we didn't use it to power a spell. We used it for another elemental. We translated that fire into an energy that we fed to the call of the approaching dragon.

Like a radio transmitter we sent Moonfire's plaintive call for her sisters out to the world.

We stayed there, holding the current in place till the force of the explosion dimmed. It seemed to last forever; forever, I stood looking around at the world lit with a soft golden glow. Forever I kept the fire back, kept it from engulfing the town. I wondered if the town could see any of this, or if it was as difficult to see as a mostly invisible dragon.

The new phoenix, the baby arisen from the ashes, flitted out of that flame, as tiny as the mouse had been. It ringed my ghostly head for another indefinite span of time as the golden glow blackened to night. Until at last I felt the sadness of parting, and a swelling of thanks.

And then it was gone.

The demon slowly collapsed us back from the sky, back from power, back from strength. Jenah and Moonfire came to a landing down on the runway of the track. I stood on the hillside in the dark, knees and elbows shivering from the prolonged stretch. For the first time in my life I felt short.

The last bits of the phoenix' explosion hung in the sky, like the aftermath of fireworks. There was fury on both the witch's and Hikari's faces, but that didn't stop them from running around and picking up bits of phoenix feathers, and occasionally kicking each other.

It was kind of nice to know that Sparkle's attention was going to be occupied for a while. I didn't think she wanted to be Kari any more than I had wanted to be like Sarmine. I remembered a girl who'd stood up for me and my stolen Bomb Pop and sighed. You never really knew anyone, not even your closest friends. Maybe not even yourself.

But self-examination would have to wait—the night wasn't over yet. Until the last bits of phoenix fire faded, the demon remained on earth.

And where he remained was in me.

Now that my adrenaline was relinquishing its hold on me, the demon's presence inside me was the most horrible thing ever. It was no longer like a goldfish swimming in my mouth. It was more like a cockroach running around behind my teeth. "If you let me stay," he said, and the words seemed to coil through the veins in my body, "then you could have this kind of power forever." With invisible fingers, he stretched us to the dragon on the field. Reached inside—and pulled a salamander off its Velcro hold on the dragon's lungs. We disintegrated the salamander. The dragon coughed, then purred.

"Am I all bad?" he said. "Look at the good we could do."

"The good you were *bound* to do," I said. "That was in your contract."

"With my help you could be greater and more powerful than all the witches in the world," he said. "Be better than Sarmine Scarabouche."

Despite the nasty slithery clattery feeling, I laughed. The gentle thanks of the phoenix still feathered my soul and I laughed—at Estahoth, the millennia-old elemental.

"Estahoth," I said. "I already am better than Sarmine Scarabouche."

And inside the cockroaches dissolved. Faded out and away. I felt Estahoth wailing, felt him clutching at his last hope of Earth.

And then he was gone.

I stared at the night sky.

Below me Jenah and Moonfire stood on the track field, watching for any sign of another dragon left in the world.

Devon stood with an arm draped on the T-Bird, looking into the night sky like he'd never seen it before. I could see why the fire elementals wanted to be on land. Earth was a beautiful place.

I parked my butt on the cement block of the T-Bird and patted its grasping claw with fingers that hardly shook. I was glad the T-Bird hadn't turned out to be the phoenix after all. No one would miss tripping over the mouse. They probably wouldn't even notice its absence.

Devon's arm was very near mine. I looked at him staring into the sky and suddenly I knew that my worries about only liking the demon-altered Devon were ridiculous. The demon might have improved his confidence, but that was only a veneer on top of the boy I liked. Like a perfect pair of jeans, or a new shade of dark-brown hair.

I set my hand on top of his. It was a few moments before I could be sure I could speak without my voice shaking or squeaking. Big important moments are funny things. You don't feel scared until it's all over and you've stopped your school from getting blown to bits by an atomic phoenix cloud.

"Are you going to be okay to play?" I said. "Your stage fright."

Devon tossed back his blond hair. "Cam, my friend," he said, "with your help I fought a demon out of my soul. I can sing in front of people."

Friend, I thought, but I didn't move my hand. All that and just *friend*. Who'd liked me, then? Was it only desperate, collar-flipping Estahoth? Shudder and sigh. "I'm glad you've got your courage back," I said.

"In more ways than one," Devon said. He got off the T-Bird and took my hands. The words came slipping out in velvety song: "She's a lion tamer, a lion tamer . . ." The song trailed off as his eyes held mine. And then shyly but firmly, he kissed me.

All I can say about that is, what seemed like ages later, I heard Jenah shout, "Woo hoo!" Reddening, we broke apart—but she was looking at the night sky, not at us.

Swooping in aerials, showing off their invisible tops and their sky-blue bellies, three dragons soared overhead.

17

Witch Girl

Blue Crush rocked.

At least, what I heard of them from outside did. The dance picked back up and Blue Crush took the stage. But I had to say a tearful farewell to an invisible-and-sky-blue dragon.

Jenah and I hugged her hard.

"She says she won't forget you," Jenah said. "She says she'll come back."

"I know," I said. Through the warmth of her hide I saw her images one last time. A picture of the three female dragons, soaring together over a long stretch of snow and ice. "Watch out for polar bears," I said.

"Tasty polar bears," said Jenah.

Behind Moonfire I saw the witch stalking up, heels grinding the dirt.

"You'd better go," I said to the dragon.

Jenah saw the approaching witch. "I'd better, too," she said, and she laid her hand on the dragon's hide one last time. "Take care."

The dragons lifted from the ground, the down-rush of wings hefting us backward. Even Sarmine stopped as the dragons rose into the night sky, translucent and winking in and out against the stars.

I kept my eyes focused on the disappearing Moonfire and pretended not to notice the witch. Of course Sarmine would never take a hint.

"No phoenix, no phoenix-burst, and Hikari back in town," said Sarmine. "All my plans destroyed. But by far, I'm the most upset about losing my dragon. That was my main source of elemental power. Was I hurting her to take her tears?"

Be firm. "It's not about that," I said, watching the stars blink. "She needed a chance to have her own life. She's not a pet."

"Well," said Sarmine. "I think it needs punishment. A grand punishment. I say three days in the dragon's garage with loss of sight and hearing. Smell, you can keep." She grabbed things from her fanny pack, crushed them in her palm, and dipped her metal wand into it.

But as she flicked her wand at me, I dipped my wooden wand into a certain sticky pear mixture and flicked back, hard.

I didn't expect her to explode like the eggplant and she didn't. But she recoiled as if she'd been punched.

Sarmine looked up at me. A strange glimmer was in her eyes.

"That era is over," I said, eye to eye. I don't think I'd realized we were the same height until just that minute. "You can't do those things to me anymore." I raised my wand as I spoke. "No more mosquito bites. No more cooked-noodle hands. No more rabid pumpkin vines."

"Is that so?"

"Yes," I said. I itched to tackle her as I had Sparkle, but I stayed calm. "And while we're on the subject, *why*? Why did you do all those horrible things?"

The witch steepled her fingers. "Horrible punishments are the established method for rearing young witches."

"Parents used to spank kids with tree branches, but that doesn't mean it's a good idea," I said.

Was that glimmer . . . pride? There was something twinkling behind her stern face. But Sarmine never smiled, and she wasn't going to start now. "Witch parents want their children to use and create antidotes. The real world is dangerous. We don't want you to be wounded—or worse—the first time another witch attacks you." Sarmine tapped her chin. "I gave you spells to learn. I've left my study door open for years, hoping you'd sneak in and find your dad's wand." She pointed at the wood-and-abalone wand I held. "Again and again I wanted you to react by using magic. But you didn't, no matter how angry I made you. You channeled all that anger into building up your story for yourself. That magical block you and Sparkle made together. I couldn't get through that."

"So the whole wicked-witch thing is what, an act?"

"Certainly not!" Sarmine said, offended. She brushed her last punishment spell to the ground and rubbed it out with her shoe. "Witches are naturally nasty," she said. "It's one of our most prized traits, along with that paranoia thing. Your father, poor soul, was never a very good witch that way. Too warmhearted about the weaklings of the world. He was always getting in my way. And yet I miss the dope like my right arm. What a weak fool I am, after all."

I nodded. Took a deep breath. "Sarmine Scarabouche," I said, "I disagree with a whole lot of the things you do. I want to live my life differently. I disagree with your choices and I want to make my own."

Sarmine's lips tightened. I could not tell at all what she thought of this statement, and I brought up my hand full of sticky pear, readying my wand again. "No witch would consider this a compliment," she said at last, "so don't take it that way." She looked down her long nose at me. "You remind me so much of your father."

I looked at the witch and then I did something I hadn't done for ten years.

I hugged her.

Slowly and stiffly, I got a hug back.

"Thanks, Mom," I said.

Appendix

SPELLS

A Verie Good Self-Defense Spell for Beginning Witches,
About Foure Years of Age

Ingredients

1. Algae
2. Hummingbird
3. Water
4. Maple Syrup
5. Cornstarch
6. Placemat
7. Harpy Claw
8. Pear
9. Paprika
10. Sugar
11. Pepper
12. Elephant Tusk

Instructions

1. Combine the 3rd and 4th ingredients at a 2:3 ratio so the amount is double the size of the ingredient that contains a human sensory organ.
2. Use twice as much of the 7th ingredient as the 12th.
3. Use 2.5 T chopped pear.
4. Substitute the 1st and 5th ingredients for the 3rd ingredient if more readily available.
5. Use one pinch of each ingredient starting with *P* that is numbered higher than 8.

6. To know the amount of the 12th ingredient, simply subtract the amount of the 11th from the amount of the 9th.

Preparation

1. If the amount of the 12th ingredient is >5, boil the 7th ingredient in a vat of chicken soup.
2. If the amount of the 4th ingredient is <=3T, chop the 8th ingredient with both hands.
3. If the amount of the 11th ingredient is greater than 4 gallons, sing "Mary Had a Little Goat" five times backward while chasing down ingredient #2.
4. Mix.

Ye Olde Demon-Loosening Spell for Feebleminded Witches Who Have Changed Their Minds About Which Puny Human Should Hold Said Demon.

Ingredients

1. Honeycomb	7. Pumpkin
2. Oyster	8. Dragon Milk
3. Apple	9. Goat's Blood
4. Paper clip	10. Dandelion Root
5. Hail	11. Earwig
6. Eggplant	12. Basilisk Urine

Instructions

1. If directed elsewhere to use #9 or #3, these are the measurements: 1 oz of #9, 2 units of #3.

2. If it is a Monday, use 1 oz of #12 and 18 units of #7. Else not, unless the date of the month adds up to 5 or is divisible by 5.

3. The amount of units of #3 plus the amount of units of #2=the amount of units of #4.

4. The item made up of chicken containers+green leafy things? Don't use that.

5. #4 is 1 greater than #3, if #5 is not used. Use 1 drop of #8, if #3 is used.

6. Use twice as many of #10 as #11; #11 is the amount of twice #3 minus the amount of #4.

7. Use all the ingredients that contain consecutive double letters, unless specified elsewhere not to.

8. #9 is imperative.

Preparation

1. If #1 is used, combine all ingredients in a cardboard box.
2. If #2 is used, combine all ingredients in a bowl.
3. If #3 is used, let it steep with #2 for twelve hours.
4. If #4 is used, speak the word "Neekwollah" twice.
5. If #5 is used, you may not breathe.
6. If #6 is used, you must chop it with a butter knife.
7. If #7 is used, you must perform the spell within a day of mixing.
8. If #8 is used, you must perform the spell within 30 seconds of mixing.
9. If #9 is used, do not touch the mixture once complete.
10. If #10 is used, gather it before the sun goes down.
11. If #11 is used, include the flower it was sitting on.
12. If #12 is used, I am very sorry for you.

ACKNOWLEDGMENTS

A long list of folks have read this book at various stages. Many thanks to Caroline M. Yoachim, Tinatsu Wallace, Meghan Sinoff, Julie McGalliard, K. Bird Lincoln, Josh English, Mischa DeNola, and my family, who all read it back when it was still called *Witch Girl Hearts Demon Boy*, as well as to more recent readers/teachers Jeff Hendriksen and Brian Allard for advising on high school things, writer/musician Spencer Ellsworth for advising on boy-band boy things, and the generally awesome Leah Cypess for advising on ways to make it generally awesome. (Any errors of non-awesomeness left would be my own.) I should also thank: anyone else I've forgotten along the way.

More thanks accrue to Tinatsu Wallace, who keeps getting thanked in subsequent books for the previous book's handmade jewelry swag (in this case, TWO baby woglets), Renee James at Powells for general event-related awesomeness, and everyone who's hosted me for *Silverblind* events, including the wonderful local libraries Ledding, Hillsdale, and St. Helens.

A really special thank-you this time to Ginger Clark, who first believed in this book; AS ALWAYS the most amazing kind of thanks to Melissa Frain for bringing out the heart of every book; Desiree Friesen for above-and-beyond efforts in publicity; Emma Goulder for the fab picture for the cover; Seth Lerner, Amy Saxon, Sarah Romeo, Karen Richardson, and the rest of the Curtis Brown and Tor Teen teams.

And finally, to my friends, family, and Eric, who continue to give me help and support, and especially to all my readers who have written me such kind words about *Ironskin* and *Copperhead* and *Silverblind*. Thank you.

November 2014
Portland, Oregon